BRIDGING
THE
ABYSS

RICHARD L. CLEARY

PRESS

BRIDGING THE ABYSS
by RICHARD L. CLEARY

Printed in the United States of America.

ISBN 9781498448703

www.xulonpress.com

DEDICATION

This book is dedicated to everyone,
whether theist or atheist,
who thinks deeply about life's
most important questions.

ACKNOWLEDGEMENTS

I wish to thank my wife Barbara and daughter Melissa Bixler for their help and suggestions in preparing this manuscript. I also wish to thank my friend and colleague Raymond Ide and my friend Byron Borger, co-owner of Hearts and Minds Bookstore, for reviewing the manuscript and for their invaluable advice and encouragement.

THE LIGHT OF THE WORLD
William Holman Hunt c.1852

"Two things fill the mind with ever new and increasing admiration and awe, the more often and steadily we reflect upon them: the starry heavens above me and the moral law within me."

Immanuel Kant

❧

"Where has God gone?" [the madman asked] "I shall tell you. We have killed him – you and I. We are his murderers. But how have we done this? How were we able to drink up the seas? Who gave us the sponge to wipe away the horizon? What did we do when we unchained the earth from its sun? Whither is it moving now? Whither are we moving now? Away from all suns? Are we not perpetually falling? Backwards, sideward, forward, in all directions? Is there any up or down left? Are we not straying as though through Infinite nothing? Has it not become colder? Is not the night closing in on us? Where is God? God is dead. God remains dead. And we have killed him. How shall we, murderers of all murderers, console ourselves?"

Friedrich Nietszche

❧

"The heart is more deceitful than all else And is desperately sick; Who can understand it?"

Jeremiah 17:9

PROLOGUE

A twelve year-old girl walking on the street near her home, in mid-afternoon, suddenly vanishes, the victim of an apparent abduction. Her disappearance sets off a chain of events which form the narrative recounted in the following pages, but before entering into that story it might be worth asking why men perpetrate such horrors. How do we explain human depravity? How can we account for the fact that moral evil seems so commonplace?

In 1948 philosopher W.T. Stace wrote an article for *The Atlantic Monthly*, a portion of which serves, perhaps, as a partial answer to these questions. Writing about the shift in the 17th century from a theistic to a materialist worldview which entailed the belief that there were no purposes or final causes in nature, Stace says:

"This, though silent and almost unnoticed, was the greatest revolution in human history, far outweighing in importance any of the political revolutions whose thunder has reverberated around the world.…

"The world, according to this new picture, is purposeless, senseless, meaningless. Nature is nothing but matter in motion. The motions of matter are governed, not by any purpose, but by blind forces and laws.…[But] if the scheme of things is purposeless and meaningless, then the life of man is purposeless and meaningless too.

Everything is futile, all effort is in the end worthless. A man may, of course, still pursue disconnected ends–money, fame, art, science–and may gain pleasure from them. But his life is hollow at the center.

"Hence, the dissatisfied, disillusioned, restless spirit of modern man....Along with the ruin of the religious vision there went the ruin of moral principles and indeed of all values....If our moral rules do not proceed from something outside us in the nature of the universe–whether we say it is God or simply the universe itself–then they must be our own inventions.

"Thus it came to be believed that moral rules must be merely an expression of our own likes and dislikes. But likes and dislikes are notoriously variable. What pleases one man, people, or culture, displeases another. Therefore, morals are wholly relative."

Bridging the Abyss should be read as a companion to my earlier novel *In the Absence of God*. Both are stories of people living in the wake of the revolution of which Stace speaks. They both offer a picture of a small slice of modern life, a glimpse of what it is to exist in a world in which people live consistently, though perhaps unwittingly, with the assumptions of modernity, chief among which is the assumption that God, if there is one, is irrelevant to our lives.

Having marginalized the God of traditional theism moderns find themselves shorn of any objective basis for forming moral judgments, for hope that the deep human yearning for justice could ever be satisfied, or for finding any ultimate meaning in the existence of the human species as a whole, or in the life of the individual in particular.

Moderns dispense with God and believe that life can go on as before, or even better than before, but this is a conceit which the sanguinary history of the 19th and 20th century confutes. A world that has abandoned God has abandoned the fountain of goodness, beauty, and truth as well as the only possible ground for belief in objective human rights or in the dignity of the individual.

Modernity has in many ways been a blessing, but it has also been a curse. History will ultimately decide whether the blessing has outweighed the curse. Meanwhile, *Bridging the Abyss* sketches the tension between these competing views of the world as they're illustrated by the lives of the characters who inhabit these pages.

I hope you enjoy the conversation.

Richard L. Cleary

2015

MAIN CHARACTERS

Carlos–Buyer of young girls

Luis–Human trafficker

Rev. Loren and Olivia Holt–Baltimore pastor and wife

Caleb and Patty Hoffmeyer–Parents of Alicia

Willis and Marie Hoffmeyer–Caleb's brother and sister-in-law

Alicia Hoffmeyer–Daughter of Caleb and Patty

Keyvon–Young mugger

John–Head of CSR

Michael–Agent of CSR

Erin–Agent of CSR

Colin–Agent of CSR

Tyrone–Agent of CSR

Danny Howe–Agent of CSR

Felix Castro–Drug/human trafficker

Enrico Gardonez–Local thug

Roberto Gardonez–Enrico's uncle

Laryssa–Michael's daughter

Julia–Michael's ex-wife

Officer Jenkins–Baltimore police officer

Cesar – Police informant

CHAPTER ONE

Three men filed slowly along a dimly lit hallway in a ramshackle ranch house ten miles southeast of the Mexican city of Cuidad Juarez just across the Rio Grande from El Paso. The house sat at the end of a dusty, unpaved road that traversed a flat, arid tract of terrain. The road consisted of little more than two tire tracks etched into the dry Mexican desert. There were no other houses or buildings of any kind within a half mile.

The hallway was lit by a single naked ceiling bulb which cast a sickly, yellowish glow on the beer cans and cigarette butts littering the floor. Old paint blistered and peeled off the faded green walls, accumulating in small heaps on a wooden floor discolored by years of accumulated coffee and beer stains.

The man in front wore a tight-fitting white T-shirt revealing a slim, muscular torso and heavily tattooed arms and neck. His head was shaved, and a confident, macho swagger marked his stride. His cold eyes were void of emotion, dissuading any attempt to establish a human connection.

His companion, a much heavier man with flabby jowls sprouting three days' stubble, walked behind drawing heavily on a cigarette. He wore an unbuttoned short-sleeved shirt that billowed over his hairy, naked paunch. Long, greasy hair hung in straggly skeins that spilled over his shoulders. He coughed, wheezed, and perspired as he made his way down the hall, as though the effort of walking pressed his stamina to its limit.

Both men were toting shoulder-holstered semi-automatic handguns.

The man in the middle, known to the others only as Carlos, was their guest. He wore cream-colored cargo pants, loafers, and an open-collared shirt. Several gold chains hung ostentatiously around his neck, their gleaming luster contrasting sharply with his tanned skin and black hair drawn back sharply into a pony-tail.

The tattooed man stopped, opened a creaky door, and stepped away allowing Carlos to see inside.

What light there was in the stuffy room filtered through a dirty window and fell in a shaft onto a bed covered with dingy gray sheets. Several children, two girls and a boy, lay dazed on the mattress, each apparently in a drug-induced stupor. Their bodies were bruised, evidently from rough treatment at the hands of their captors, and each was tied securely by one wrist to a bedpost. None of them looked older than thirteen or fourteen, perhaps even younger. The room stank of sweat and urine. Buzzing flies ricocheted off the dirty window panes and circled lazily about the room, occasionally alighting on the children's faces.

The guest studied the three children for a few moments then nodded with his eyes. The tattooed man closed the door and moved on to the next door in the hallway. Carlos peered into the room from the open doorway and witnessed a similar scene. Two children, both young girls wearing plain shifts, lay on a grimy mattress with one wrist tethered to the bedstead, their eyes bloodshot and empty. Their bodies appeared bruised, and blood stained the shift of one of the girls. She appeared to have been sexually assaulted.

Carlos turned and looked at Tattoo with an arched eyebrow. Tattoo cocked his head and formed his mouth into a humorless smirk as if to acknowledge that he knew what his guest was thinking and that indeed it was he who was responsible for the girl's condition, and, moreover, he had no regrets.

The trio started back toward the living room, but Carlos paused and asked what was in a third room across from the one they'd just visited.

"That's not for sale, *amigo*," the fat man answered.

"Just want to window shop." Carlos replied.

Fat man shot a quick look at Tattoo who nodded slightly. Fat Man opened the door, and Carlos was surprised to see a girl, also about twelve, lying on a soiled bed. She was clearly an Anglo with blondish hair. Her eyes were open, but she didn't seem to take notice of the man in the doorway. One wrist was manacled to the bed frame, her clothes were disheveled, her hair was matted and tangled, and her eyes looked like they'd been doing a lot of crying. Unlike the others, however, she didn't appear to have been physically abused.

Carlos lifted his brows in a gesture of interest. "How much for this one?"

"Not for sale," Tattoo repeated in Spanish.

"My patron would like very much to place a bid, I'm quite sure," Carlos countered. He took out his phone and held it up to snap a photo of the dazed girl on the bed.

"No pictures," Fat Man commanded sharply, placing his hand roughly on Carlos' arm. Carlos assured him that, given his patron's taste for young blond girls, he might make an offer that'd be very hard to decline.

The two associates glanced at each other, and Tattoo, who was clearly in charge, motioned slightly with his head and eyes as if to grant permission for the photos.

Carlos snapped off a couple of shots, one a close-up of the girl's face and her hollow, vacant eyes, the other a zoomed-out frame showing her lying on the bed to which she was tied. He immediately texted the pics to his patron with the message that the girl wasn't for sale, but that the businessmen with whom he was dealing might change their minds for the right price.

❦

Loren Holt sat on the living room sofa with Caleb and Patty Hoffmeyer in their neat brick home on a tree-lined street in Baltimore, Maryland. The neighborhood in which the Hoffmeyers resided was only a couple of blocks removed from one of the poorest, most crime-intensive precincts of the city. Holt was quietly holding Patty's hands in his. No one had said much of anything for the last hour, nor had the Hoffmeyers been able to get more than a few brief snatches of sleep in the past three nights.

Three days earlier a call had come to Loren at his office in the church he served as pastor from a couple in his congregation who were requesting a visit. They were clearly distraught. Fighting to keep control of his emotions, Caleb related to Loren over the phone that their twelve-year old daughter, Alicia, had left home in the afternoon to attend a friend's birthday party just a short distance from their home, but she never arrived at the party and seemed to have completely vanished.

The police were committing a lot of manpower to the search, the FBI had been brought in, and all the known pedophiles in the city were being checked out. Volunteers had scoured the area, but no sign of the young girl had been discovered except her cell phone which her abductors, if she had indeed been abducted, had doubtless discarded so it wouldn't be used to locate her.

Holt, a slim man in his late-forties with a full head of wavy dark hair parted in the middle and graying at the temples, had been with the couple for much of the time since their daughter's disappearance. The anguish the Hoffmeyers bore was draining their emotional reserves and crushing their spirit. They fought hard to avoid becoming hysterical, but whenever they thought of what might have happened to the child who was their whole life the tears flowed, and their strength drained from them as though their bones had turned to powder.

Alicia was their only child. She had had a younger sister whom they'd lost three years before to a childhood cancer, and now they were frightened to the point of panic that Alicia was also lost to someone who was doing unimaginable things to her.

The thought of their innocent little girl's terror and the pain she may be suffering, coupled with their own helplessness, was at times more than they could endure, which is why Loren, despite his own exhaustion, and Caleb and Patty's insistence that he get some rest, couldn't bring himself to leave them.

Everyone in the house–which as of that morning included Caleb Hoffmeyer's brother Willis, a literature professor at a local community college, and his wife Marie who worked for a social agency–was emotionally spent. Tears no longer came quite as easily as during the first two days. The police confessed they had nothing at all to go on. Shock, grief, and despair filled the Hoffmeyer home like a cold, tenebrous pall. There was nothing to be done but pray, and Caleb and Patty had been doing that almost non-stop from the beginning.

The Hoffmeyers were both in their mid-thirties. Caleb was a tall, trim, athletic man with curly, sand-colored hair who enjoyed distance running. He was a project manager for an engineering firm in the city. Patty was a slender, attractive, blondish woman who worked as a dental hygienist. They'd been members of Loren's church for about ten years, and active in the church's ministry to the city's disadvantaged communities.

Loren wished there was something he could say that would afford them some measure of comfort, but he was not a man given to mouthing platitudes, and he knew there was nothing else that could be offered to these despondent parents other than a hand to hold and a shoulder to cry on. He chose to say little beyond praying with them.

Shortly after noon the oppressive atmosphere pervading the Hoffmeyer home was pierced by the peal of the doorbell. Everyone in the house, having grown accustomed to the funereal quiet, was startled by the sound. Willis rose slowly from his armchair to answer, expecting a family friend come to offer support to his brother and sister-in-law.

He was surprised to find two men standing at the door who didn't look at all like friends or acquaintances of the family. Both men wore aviator sunglasses and overcoats against the chill late-November air. One was a tall, fortyish African-American, and the other a slightly older, shorter man, balding and thickly built. They looked like police.

"Can I help you?"

"We'd like to speak with Mr. and Mrs. Hoffmeyer if we may," the shorter man replied.

Willis turned to his brother seated on the sofa to see if he agreed to talk to these men. Caleb nodded, and Willis stepped aside, tacitly inviting them to enter.

The front door opened into a modest, but tastefully furnished living room. Loren and Caleb stood as the two visitors moved a couple of steps into the room.

"I'm Caleb Hoffmeyer, and this is my wife, Patty. Who are you? Are you police?"

The shorter man removed his sunglasses. "No, we're not police, Mr. Hoffmeyer. My name's John. My associate's name is Michael. We're affiliated with an organization that tracks down and tries to free children who've been sold into sex slavery."

"Sex slavery?" Patty cried in alarm. "Why are you *here*?" She was very afraid she already knew the answer.

Caleb wanted to ask for some kind of identification, but before he could get the words out John was talking again. He had a soft, avuncular voice that was soothingly reassuring. He directed his attention toward Patty.

"We have a team that's had a house just across the Mexican border under surveillance for the last few days, Mrs. Hoffmeyer. We were able to electronically intercept a texted photo of a young Anglo girl being kept in the house. Most of the kids there are Hispanic so when we saw this one it kinda' jumped out at us. We ran it through a missing persons data base and thought it matched a picture of your daughter. Is this her?"

He took his phone out of his pocket, brought up the photo, and handed it to Caleb.

"Oh, God," Caleb exclaimed softly as he passed the phone to Patty who became almost frantic. It was indeed Alicia, and she looked awful. Her hollow, stupefied eyes and general appearance filled Patty with heartbreak and horror. She buried her face in Caleb's chest and sobbed.

"You know where she is? Have you contacted the police? What are you going to do?" A dozen questions surged into Caleb's mind simultaneously, and he rushed them out without waiting for the answers.

"Well, we can't contact the police in Mexico since most of them in that area are probably taking bribes from the people who're holding your daughter. She's in a house outside a small town...."

"It's only been three days," Caleb interrupted. "How did they get her there so fast? How did they get her across the border?"

"We're pretty sure these are professional human traffickers," John answered. "Getting her across the border wasn't a problem for them. How they got her there so fast .... they probably used a plane. But she's alive and we're going to try to get her back for you."

For the first time in three days, the Hoffmeyers felt a faint glimmer of hope begin to flicker to life in their hearts.

"How are you going to do that?"

"I'm sorry, but we can't talk about that."

"Do you have authority to operate in Mexico?" Willis asked.

"Can't talk about that either. What I can tell you is that we're going to have to move soon. We wanted to talk to you because we understand what you must be going through, and we wanted to confirm that the girl in the photo is Alicia. We also wanted to let you know that she's still alive."

What he didn't say, but what he thought to himself was, "for now."

"We're going to have to ask you to trust us. I also have to emphasize that it's important that none of you contact the Baltimore police or the FBI. If you do they may interfere in such a way as to prevent us from extracting your daughter, or in some way inadvertently tipping off the people holding her."

This request raised suspicions. Caleb and Patty looked at each other as if seeking some sort of confirmation each from the other that these men were to be trusted. Their explanation of who they were and what sort of work they did sounded alien and strange, but they were desperate. Turning to the man who had done all the talking, Caleb asked, "How soon?"

"We'll be in touch tomorrow. Maybe tonight. Probably by phone, but we're staying in town so we might stop by. In any case, we'll let you know as soon as we hear from our people in Mexico."

The Hoffmeyers decided to give them until the next day before they notified the FBI of the photo, but they didn't know how they would bear the suspense of waiting.

"It doesn't matter what time it is. As soon as you know something, please call us." Caleb gave the men his cell number.

The men nodded, emphasized again the importance of keeping the information confidential, handed Caleb a business card, and left. The printing on the card said simply **Capital Search and Rescue** with a cell phone number. There was nothing else, no website, no email, no office address.

Once their enigmatic visitors had departed everyone stood staring at each other in stunned surprise. Nobody knew quite what to say. Marie and Patty hugged. At length Caleb asked Loren if he thought these men were being honest with them or if he and his wife were being set up for some sort of scam by people who prey upon the bereaved.

"If they were legitimate why didn't they even have a website?" He wondered aloud.

Loren suppressed his reservations and replied that it didn't seem as if Caleb and Patty had much choice but to trust them, at least until tomorrow, and suggested that it might be a good idea to pray some more. As everyone else bowed their heads, Willis and Marie quietly slipped into the kitchen to make tea.

Caleb and Patty were afraid to let their expectations rise too high. They didn't want to start rejoicing only to be visited with tragic news the next day. Yet they couldn't help but yield to the hope that their prayers were being answered.

Once the prayers ended, Loren wandered into the kitchen to pour a cup of tea, passing Marie on her way out with a tray of cookies and tea for Caleb and Patty. He smiled grimly and politely, an expression of empathy for the Hoffmeyers' suffering, but Marie's response was decidedly cool. Loren noticed the chill but chose not to assign any significance to it.

Willis set out a cup and saucer for Loren who placed a tea bag in the cup while Willis poured hot water from the pot. Willis was two years older than his brother but looked a lot like him. He was tall, lanky, and clean-shaven with longish, light-colored hair, a few undisciplined shocks of which stuck out at angles, like flames struggling to rise free of his head. He had a strong, straight nose which supported wire-rimmed glasses behind which were a pair of piercing greenish-brown eyes.

"You'll have to excuse me from the prayers, Reverend. I don't believe there's anyone out there listening."

Holt was a little taken aback by Willis' candor, though not so much that he let his surprise show. He thanked him for pouring the water, but said nothing in reply to his profession of skepticism. He stood pressing a spoon against the tea bag with an expression on his face that invited Willis to continue.

"This isn't the time to talk about it, I guess, and I certainly don't want to upset Caleb and Patty, but I just don't see how anyone living in the modern age can seriously think there's a God out there who cares about what happens to us. If there were why would he let something like Alicia's kidnapping happen? Please don't take any of this personally."

Despite Willis' request not to construe his words as a personal insult, it was hard to miss the contempt for the belief that was the guiding principle of Loren's life that they conveyed.

Loren smiled and shook his head softly as if to assure Willis that he took no offense. He tactfully, if not entirely truthfully, replied that he didn't take it personally at all.

Willis seemed to want to talk about his objections to Loren's religion further, but was reluctant to do so under the present circumstances. Even so, he felt the need to explain himself at least somewhat. Moving toward the stove to set the kettle back on the burner he offered an off-handed explanation. "I just don't see how it's possible to believe in such things in an age of science and technology, in an age when Darwin, or at least his discovery, has made God unnecessary." There was a hint of resignation, almost wistfulness, in his voice. "I know my brother and Patty believe that, and I did, too, as a child, but I can't believe it now. I've outgrown it."

Holt smiled thinly and raised the cup to his lips to blow across the steaming tea. The implied inference in Willis' remark, he supposed, was that people who *hadn't* outgrown it were emotionally and intellectually still juveniles.

"I wonder," Loren said finally as he lowered his cup, "if when primitive man learned to use the wheel, he said that now, in this age of technological advance, it's no longer possible to believe in God."

He flicked his eyebrows, smiled and walked back into the living room stirring his cup, leaving Willis a little miffed. He thought Holt's curt reply was a bit of a put-down, though in fact Holt had not intended it that way.

Willis was a kind, soft-spoken man whose attitude toward religion in general, and Christianity in particular, was rather complicated. In the abstract he considered religious belief to be at best a symptom of a mild mental disorder and at worst, toxic. Nevertheless, he exempted from this low opinion individual Christians such as his parents, his brother, and his sister-in-law because he loved and respected them, but Loren Holt was a different matter. To be treated flippantly by a preacher, a breed he placed on the same plane as carnival barkers, or con-men who prey upon the gullible, was an affront which, despite his gentle demeanor, he felt obliged to answer if ever an opportunity presented itself.

It wasn't so much the abrasion suffered by his pride that obligated him, although there was some of that, but rather a sense of what was almost a moral duty. He was impelled by a conviction that Holt, by virtue of the fact that he was a Christian pastor, in addition to being impertinent, was *ipso facto* intellectually irresponsible and ignorant, and it was incumbent upon him, Willis felt, to help this cleric see plainly both his intellectual inadequacies and his need for enlightenment.

Willis and Caleb were raised in a devout family, descended from Mennonite stock, on a dairy farm in central Pennsylvania. The brothers were very close and spent a lot of time together while growing up, but when Willis went away to college at the age of seventeen something changed. On his trips home he no longer would accompany the family to church, a development which deeply troubled his parents. They couldn't bear to watch their son abandon so much that they held precious. They tried to talk to him about it, but were ill-equipped to answer the kind of scientific and philosophical objections he was absorbing at his school, and which he, lovingly and respectfully, posed to them. Finally, they just agreed not to talk about his religious doubts at all.

For the elder Hoffmeyers their faith was their life, and Willis' rejection of it was almost indistinguishable, in their minds, from a rejection of them. He assured them it most certainly was not, but even so, Willis' drift toward unbelief was a terrible blow which caused them to feel increasingly estranged from their son.

His was a familiar story in families across the country. In college he was confronted with a host of challenges to his childhood beliefs, challenges his church had done very little to prepare him for. Professors and friends confronted him with attacks on his faith that he was simply incapable of refuting. The persistent battering to which his youthful creed was subjected in the lecture hall and in the dorm room wore him down, but the most corrosive influence on his religious convictions was that every person he encountered whose intelligence he admired was either unimpressed by his religious beliefs or openly hostile to them.

He was by turns distressed that other Christians seemed just as impotent in the face of similar challenges as he was, disdainful of the apparent intellectual inadequacy and incoherence of their responses, and seduced by the various hedonistic enticements of college life. Reinforcing his growing sense of alienation from the faith of his family was the repellant religious dogmatism of a dorm mate who insisted that Willis would face an eternity of hell-fire if he abjured the faith. Willis thought it almost amusing that this fellow, whom he judged to be about as sensitive as a fence post, would proclaim that God was a God of love one moment and in the next breath declare that this God of love delighted in afflicting people with eternal torment.

By the end of his sophomore year he simply decided that he no longer believed any of it. At first he hid his new-found skepticism from his family, but by the middle of his junior year he "came out" as an atheist to his parents over the Christmas holiday. Though they had recognized that matters were trending in that direction, they were nevertheless devastated, and Caleb, who always looked up to his older brother, and who was in the middle of his freshman year at a different school, was also saddened but not surprised. He was seeing it happen to students at his school as well.

Caleb and Willis remained close despite having a diminishing number of common interests, and the two even took jobs in the same city—which was actually a coincidence—but there was always a wall between them, like the clear plexiglass barrier in jails that separates prisoners from their visitors.

Their father had passed away five years previous to the events of this week, and their mother had sold the family farm and moved to Illinois to live with their sister and her family. It was difficult for her to make it back to Baltimore when she got the call from Patty about Alicia, but she was in touch daily by phone and text messages.

Apart from when he was with Caleb and Patty, Willis was accustomed to being surrounded by people who believed as he did and was also accustomed to a certain deference from students awed by his academic achievements. Holt, however, was obviously not impressed with Willis' credentials, and although Willis was not a man particularly given to vanity he considered Holt's response to him a kind of intellectual *lèse majesty* and a throwing down of the gauntlet, as it were.

But now was not the proper time to cross swords with Holt. Willis pushed the perceived slight from his mind and rejoined the others in the living room.

Carlos was ushered by Fat Man and Tattoo into what passed for the sitting room of the dilapidated *hacienda*. A few chairs and a threadbare sofa stood against the walls. A table and two more chairs were situated toward the middle of the room. The floor was partially covered with a rumpled carpet that had evidently suffered years of abuse.

A man seated at the table leaned back in his chair, eyeing Carlos for some indication of his degree of interest in his merchandise. Two burly *hombres* stood close-by.

"Well, *señor* Carlos. What do you think of my little flowers, eh?" The man at the table was speaking. He was of medium height, a little overweight, well-dressed with oily black hair combed straight back, a thin goatee and lots of jewelry on his hands, ears, and neck. He was clearly *El Jefe*. He seemed, at least superficially, to be an affable fellow whose eyes danced when he spoke.

"*Muy bien*," Carlos replied. "My client will be very interested in what you have for sale, especially the Anglo girl. How much are you asking for her?"

"I cannot guarantee you that the Anglo girl will be for sale, *señor*." This was said with an expression of sympathetic regret which was entirely insincere. "As for the rest, that will be decided later. You know there are other interested parties, and the bidding begins at four. There are five items up for auction. I would guess that they'll go for anywhere from ten to twenty thousand U.S dollars. Apiece. Bring cash, *por favor*." This the man said with a convivial grin as though he were discussing an auction of bottles of wine.

Carlos knew the procedure. It had been explained to him by Fat Man earlier. Smiling, he nodded to *El Jefe*, turned and walked toward the front door. He placed his hand on the doorknob and turned back to the man sitting at the table. "I'll be bringing a van. I'll need the space." Smiling again, he opened the door and left.

CHAPTER TWO

Their hopes buoyed by word that Alicia was still alive and that a rescue operation was underway, Caleb and Patty felt they needed to get out of the house. For three days they could scarcely summon the will to move across the room, but now they decided to go for a walk and get some fresh air. They invited the others to stay and make themselves at home while they were gone.

The grey, overcast November skies suited their state of mind. The last three nights had been a torment. They couldn't sleep for worrying, and when in the early morning hours they would doze off for a few minutes they'd suddenly be jolted awake by horrid nightmares.

When they rose in the morning their first thought was of their daughter and the terrors she might have suffered or was suffering. The realization that she was gone swept over them in icy waves, sapping their bodies of both will and strength. The fear that assaulted them as soon as sleep abandoned them gave way to a struggle to get up from their bed and face the tedium of sitting around the house hour after hour awaiting word from the police. To be caught in the grip of despair as soon as they were conscious made them physically ill. Their first acts of the new day were either to burst into tears or to try to suppress nausea, or both.

Adding to their despondency was the realization that the memory of their daughter's face was slipping away from them after only just a few days of her absence and that it might soon be difficult to remember her appearance without looking at a photo.

All of this was taking its toll on their emotional well-being and even their relationship with each other. They'd always had a strong marriage, but anxiety and lack of sleep were making them both irritable and impatient, and they struggled with the inclination to take it out on each other.

They were deeply grateful for the support of friends, but it was awkward sitting silently with visitors when there was nothing left to say. Now the visit of these men from CSR was like a beam of sunshine poking through the gloom. It would be good to get out of the house, drink in the late autumn afternoon, and try to relax in the comfort of each other's love and the hope that God would somehow get them through this terrible time.

Loren felt ill at ease staying at the Hoffmeyer house and decided that now would be a good time to head back to his office. Willis had an afternoon class and decided to remain at his brother's until it was time to leave for the college.

Marie would drop him off at school, do some shopping, and pick him up after class was over. She was Willis' second wife and he her second husband. The first go-around went badly for both of them. In Willis' case he'd made a reckless decision, based more on physical attraction than common sense. A year or so into the union the truth of Dickens' observation in *David Copperfield* that "There's no disparity in marriage like unsuitability in intellect and purpose" was being regularly impressed upon him. Indeed, he felt like he was Copperfield married to Dora, but unlike Copperfield, he foresaw that to be so unequally yoked wasn't going to work out for either of them. He applied to his own circumstance Evelyn Waugh's pungent description of a failed marriage in *Brideshead Revisited* in which Waugh has one of his characters declare that he, "suddenly knew that he had no longer any desire, or tenderness, or esteem for a once-beloved wife; no pleasure in her company, no wish to please, no curiosity about anything she might ever do or say or think; no hope of setting things right, no self-reproach for the disaster." This state of affairs being clearly recognized by both Willis and his wife, they agreed to dissolve their relationship.

Marie's first husband was simply a lout, and her marriage to him lasted two years before she realized that things would never improve. She didn't want the rest of her life to be a living hell, so she left him.

A year or so later Marie and Willis met through the intercession of mutual friends. They dated for another year and ultimately agreed to chance a second marriage. It seemed a good match. Most successful marriages are partnerships, some are even companionships. Theirs was both.

Their union was childless, however, so Willis doted on Caleb's girls. He was profoundly embittered by the death of their second daughter and couldn't understand how Caleb and Patty could continue to believe in God after she died. Throughout her illness their commitment and trust never wavered, and when she passed their faith survived even amidst their profound grief. Willis thought this as astonishing as it was senseless.

Loren retrieved his jacket and move quietly toward the door, but Marie surprised him by speaking to him.

"You're leaving? Well, then, I suppose my question will have to wait."

Marie had scarcely acknowledged his presence until now and he was startled that she had spoken to him and even more that she wanted to ask him something.

Willis had been on his laptop googling *Capital Search and Rescue* to learn what he could about the people his brother was dealing with. He couldn't find much on CSR, but he did learn that there were a number of organizations doing work similar to what CSR was engaged in. Even so, there was no mention of the methods they used to find and free the children they sought to rescue.

He next did a search on "sex slavery" and began reading off the statistics to Marie. To his mild surprise there were millions of victims worldwide, many of them young girls put to work as prostitutes in the U.S., some "surgically" stitched after having been raped to make them seem like virgins, others used in child pornography, still others enslaved to wealthy businessmen and sheiks overseas. Like most people, neither Willis nor Marie was aware of the full magnitude of the problem, a problem that spanned the entire globe.

Loren paused on his way to the door. "What question is that, Marie?"

Marie had been momentarily distracted by the welter of statistics Willis was rattling off and paused to listen to her husband's recitation, peering over his shoulder at the computer screen. She had intended to ask Loren how his God could let such horrors happen, but what passed her lips was actually a rather different question.

"Why do men do such horrible things?" It was half-whispered as she gazed at the screen, directed to no one in particular, and evidently rhetorical, but Loren chose to offer an answer anyway.

Looking first at Willis and then at Marie as he put on his jacket, he said matter-of-factly, "Probably they do it because they *can*, Marie. If they want to there's no reason not to, if they can get away with it."

Marie appeared stunned by what she heard Holt say. She was a tall, thin woman with short brown hair who had the rather disconcerting habit of rolling her eyes toward the top of her head when addressing someone while mildly agitated.

"No reason not to?" Marie's voice was just a decibel or two shy of a shout. What she interpreted as a frivolous response from the pastor was inexcusably insensitive, and she was visibly struggling to suppress an emotional explosion. Her eyelids fluttered as her pupils disappeared somewhere behind them.

"How about the fact that it's a crime against civilization and humanity, Mr. Holt? How about the fact that these girls are wrecked, mentally, emotionally, and usually physically, for the rest of their lives? Doesn't that matter to you, sir?" The more she said the more she seethed. Her face was flushed and her hands were trembling. She fought to maintain her self-control.

Loren's disarming smile soothed her but little.

"Please, call me Loren."

At first Marie thought that Holt was callously excusing these reprehensible crimes, but she realized she shouldn't be too hasty to draw conclusions about his intent. Even so, neither she nor her husband understood why this clergyman had said what he just had. Surely, he wasn't joking since no one could be so stupid as to make light of these things in the home of a family undergoing such tragedy. They stared at him, wordlessly demanding an explanation.

"Of course I care about those girls, Marie," Loren said calmly, "but the point is if men can get away with doing what they do to them, why shouldn't they commit whatever crimes they wish? If there's no punishment, no accountability to anyone, then what does it mean to say that it's 'wrong' for them to do it?"

Marie fumbled for an answer, but couldn't immediately produce one.

"You see," he continued softly when neither of them seemed prepared to answer his question, "something can only be wrong if there's a moral authority that establishes the moral laws of the universe and holds us accountable to them. If there's no such authority, as presumably both of you believe, then right and wrong refer to nothing more than what people like and don't like. Morality is in the eye of the beholder."

At this juncture Willis spoke up, "You think that if you believe in God you'll do right, and if you don't you won't? That strikes me as preposterous given the history of religion in the world."

"No, Willis, that's not what I'm saying at all. I'm not saying that if you believe in God you'll do what's right, or even *know* what's right. I'm saying that unless God exists there is no real *moral* right or wrong in the first place. There are just things that people do. What's wrong is simply what's out of fashion. What's right is arbitrary and based on custom or the tastes of the social and cultural elite.

"You're a literature professor so I'm sure you've read Nietzsche. He said that, 'For the man of knowledge there are no moral duties.' What he meant was that for the man who knows there is no God, morality is only a non-binding subjective preference."

Willis was disdainful of Loren's explanation, but he tried to keep it from showing. "Morality can exist without God just as mathematics can, Pastor. God's not necessary for people to know what's right and wrong."

Loren stepped away from the door and back into the room. He didn't think the analogy with mathematics was a good one. In his mind, if there were no God there'd be neither morality *nor* mathematics, but he chose to reply in a different vein. "Math is descriptive, Willis. It tells us how the world is. Morality is descriptive, too. It tells us how people behave, but it's also *pre*scriptive. It tells us how we *should* behave. It imposes obligations on us to behave in certain ways. Math imposes no duties. If one violates a mathematical principle he's made an error, but he's not really *guilty* of anything. He's transgressed no duty to anyone.

"If you're right, though, and if atheism is true, then everything we do is determined by the laws of nature. Nothing could have been otherwise, and if it couldn't have been otherwise then guilt and regret are illusions and moral outrage makes no sense. There's no reason to pay any attention to any of it. The men who abducted Alicia have no reason to care about any feelings of guilt they may have nor any reason to regret what they did, as long as they don't get caught, and our moral outrage at what they did is out of place. It presupposes that things could have been other than they are, but if it's all determined by nature then how could they have been otherwise? "

"Guilt and regret are part of our evolutionary heritage," Marie interjected, her eyes spinning upward like the pictures in a slot machine and her outrage having subsided to mere indignation, "they've evolved for good reason, just like our instincts, so certainly we should heed them."

"I don't know about that, Marie. Just because something has evolved is no reason why we should heed it. If the human experience of guilt has evolved then so has the human yearning for God, but you don't believe that that yearning corresponds to anything real, and presumably you don't think people should heed *it*."

The room was quiet. Willis and Marie didn't quite know how to respond to what Holt had just said. Loren smiled and told them that he was glad to have met them, a pleasantry which was entirely sincere, though he wished their meeting had been under less tragic circumstances. Adding that he hoped to see them again, he zipped up his jacket, opened the front door and walked out into the damp, chilly afternoon.

As he drove down the street on his way to the church he passed Patty and Caleb strolling slowly hand in hand, returning from their walk. He waved to them and shouted that he'd stop back later that night. They nodded and returned the wave. Not many words had passed between them during their outing around the neighborhood. They were content to be sharing their grief alone, listening to the chitter of the sparrows and soaking in the sweet smell of damp, decaying autumn leaves which filled the air. As they turned a corner onto their street Patty raised her eyes toward her husband and quietly whispered that she didn't know if she'd be able to survive bad news about Alicia. It was almost more than she could bear to lose Sarah, their younger daughter, and now to have Alicia taken from her would, she was very sure, completely drain her of her will to go on living.

Her husband let her hand slip from his, wrapped his arm around her shoulder, and pulled her close to himself. He had wondered often over the last few days why tragedy seems to be visited in greater measure upon some people than others. It seemed so unfair. Like Patty, he feared that losing Alicia would be a blow from which he would never recover, yet he knew that right now Patty wanted and needed him to be strong.

He gave her a squeeze and said, "I know, honey. I feel the same way, but let's not think about losing her, let's not give up yet. Let's just trust that God won't let the world hand us more pain than we can endure."

Caleb closed his eyes and let out a deep sigh. His faith and Patty's had been tested almost to the breaking point when they lost Sarah, but it nevertheless survived. He silently prayed that it would survive this trial, too.

❧

A white Dodge van trundled up the dirt road toward the Mexican *hacienda*, churning up billows of dust in its wake. The day was unusually warm for this time of year, even for the hot Sonoran climate. Carlos parked the van about twenty yards from the front porch and checked his watch while sauntering up to the house. It was 3:45 p.m. Mountain time.

Carlos was in his mid-thirties, handsome, and athletically built. His white shirt was opened down to his sternum allowing the gold chains adorning his neck to highlight the light bronze of his skin and complement the gold band of his wrist watch. He carried a black satchel bulging with crisp $100 bills.

Several other vehicles were parked in front of the house which meant that other buyers were already inside.

As he approached the porch the two burly bodyguards he noted earlier emerged armed with shotguns from the *hacienda* and wordlessly frisked him for weapons.

Having passed inspection he entered the building and joined a group of men loitering in the living room. Fat Man was there with

El Jefe, who was passing out drinks, but Tattoo was not. There were three other buyers, all carrying valises, presumably full of cash, and looking mildly nervous. They were a diverse group–a Middle-Easterner, an Asian, and a European.

Carlos smiled genially at the others who scarcely acknowledged his presence. "Some lovely blossoms to delight us this afternoon, eh?" His attempt at affability was met with little more than a few grunts. None of them were there to make friends and they weren't interested in schmoozing.

El Jefe, whose name, it transpired, was Luis, bid everyone sit. They took chairs that had been arranged in a semi-circle around the center of the room. Luis stood in the entrance to a hall that led back to the bedrooms toward the rear of the house.

After some introductory instructions on how the bidding would proceed, Tattoo appeared in the entrance with one of the Hispanic girls. She was very young, eleven or twelve, and obviously terrified. Her face was red and swollen from crying. She was barefoot and wearing only a light shift. Tattoo walked her to the center of the room to facilitate inspection by the buyers. Her hair hung in her face but it didn't conceal the fear in her eyes.

Carlos placed his elbows on the arms of the chair, crossed his right leg over his left, and laced his fingers together as he looked the girl over. When the bidding commenced he entered the competition with an offer of $3000.

As afternoon stretched into evening other friends and family of the Hoffmeyers stopped by the house with food and support.

After his slightly uncomfortable discussion with Willis and Marie, Pastor Holt headed for his office where he hoped to spend a few hours getting caught up on church business. He worked until dark, which arrived around 5:30, left the church and walked next door to his home for dinner. As he arrived at the front of his house he recalled an evening similar to this one two decades ago when he was walking on the same part of the street in front of his home. His memory of the scene seized him with such vivacity that it was as if it were occurring all over again.

He remembered three young men wearing hoodies swaggering up to him just as he reached his front steps on that night all those years ago.

"Hey, man. This is our street. You ain't 'lowed to be walkin' on it 'less you pay a toll," one of the boys informed him.

Holt ignored the boy, who couldn't have been more than thirteen, and tried to by-pass the trio, but the just-barely teenager moved to block his way. Loren began to suspect this encounter was not going to end well, and felt anxiety creeping over him. His assailants, he realized, hadn't shown their hands which they kept shoved down in their pockets, leading him to suspect that they were concealing weapons.

"Toll's ten bucks, man. Time to pay up."

"Look, fellas, I'm not going to give you anything," Holt replied calmly. "If you want money you can stop by the church tomorrow, and I'll give you work to do, and you can earn some cash, but I'm not giving you any. Now excuse me." With that he tried to push his way through to the porch steps.

Almost instantly he felt like he'd been struck on the side of the head with a hammer. Flashes went off in his brain and the next thing he knew he was laying in the street, conscious but too dazed to move.

When he finally recovered himself enough to sit up he checked his pockets and found his wallet missing. That discovery made him feel even worse than the blow to the head. The hassle of having to stop his credit cards, getting his driver's license replaced, and, he realized with a cold feeling in the pit of his stomach, getting a new social security number, since his old card was in his wallet as well, made him physically sick.

He retched in the street and then staggered into the house holding the side of his head. When his wife Olivia saw his condition and heard his explanation of what had happened she was frantic, alternating between solicitous pity and barely-contained fury. Loren was eventually able to assure her that he wasn't seriously injured despite the knot that was swelling on the side of his skull. Olivia calmed down a little, but only temporarily.

Once she was satisfied her husband was not going to die her thoughts turned to her children and her anger rekindled. The children were still very young at that time, but they'd be starting school soon.

"How can we send our kids to a school where they'll be confronted with people like those thugs everyday? We can't have our kids scared to go to school, Loren. If they go to the schools that service this neighborhood they're going to be bullied and mistreated, or worse. We owe it to them to send them to a decent school where they can get a good education and don't have to be fearful."

There really wasn't anything Loren could say in reply to Olivia's impassioned case, but they had chosen to accept a call at their church because they wanted to minister where there was real need, and a couple of blocks over there was certainly real need. The adjacent neighborhood was riddled with drugs, crime, fragmented families, and poverty, and too often it spilled over, as it did that evening, into their own neighborhood.

They were well aware, too, that they couldn't truly minister to people unless they lived in their community and sent their kids to school with the kids who lived there. Commuting from the suburbs was not likely to make for an effective ministry. Enrolling their kids in a private school half-way across the city would send the wrong message. It's hard to convince people you care about them if, as their pastor, you don't want to live and go to school among them.

"You're right about the school, hon," Loren replied, holding an ice pack to his head. "Maybe we should just start our own school. I can't think of a better way to make a difference here than to offer parents a good educational environment for their kids. What d'ya think?"

Olivia threw up her hands in exasperation. It was not the answer she was hoping to hear, but it was pretty much the sort of answer she expected from her husband.

Later that evening the doorbell rang. The swelling on Loren's head had subsided substantially, and he got up from his desk where he'd been busying himself constructing a list of everyone he'd need to call the next day to protect his already tenuous financial affairs and went to answer it. He was surprised to see a young teenager in a hoodie standing on the porch.

"Can I help you?"

"Yeah. I brung ya' this." The boy thrust out his hand which held Loren's wallet.

Holt was momentarily speechless but recovered quickly and invited the boy in.

The young man seemed reluctant, but he overcame his reservations, stepped into the Holts' living room, and explained himself.

"What happened tonight, wan't right. I din't want it to happen, and the guys said it wouldn't, but then they went and did it anyways."

"Yes, they certainly did," Loren agreed sardonically.

The boy was clearly uncomfortable in Holt's living room and looked everywhere but at Holt as he spoke. "Yeah. Well, I want you to know I din't do none of it, but when you was knocked down and the other guys boosted your stuff we ran to my friend's house, and when we got there I told 'em it was wrong, and said I wanted to take the wallet back. They din't want to, and they took the money outa' it and threw it onna table. I grabbed it, and brung it here, 'cause it was wrong to hit you and take it an' all."

Loren reflected for a moment. He was deeply relieved to have the wallet and its contents back. The money was about thirty dollars, which was a lot on their budget, but they could survive without it. Although he would have liked to know who the boys were who assaulted him and took his money, he didn't want to put this boy in the position of "ratting out" his friends.

"What's your name?"

"Keyvon."

"Well, Keyvon, You did a very good thing bringing this wallet back. It took a lot of character and courage to do it, and it shows that you're a fine young man with a good heart. I hope you remember this every time in your life you're tempted to do something your conscience tells you is wrong. Remember that you're a good person. Always do what your conscience tells you is right, even when it's hard. The more times you do what's right the easier it gets, and the better man you'll be."

Keyvon looked down at the floor and didn't say anything.

"I told your friends I wasn't going to give them any money, so they took it from me. By returning my wallet you've saved me an awful lot of trouble."

He beckoned to Olivia to bring her purse to him out of which he retrieved two ten dollar bills. "This is for being an honest person and returning my wallet."

Keyvon demurred, but Loren stuffed the bills into the pocket of his hoodie.

"I also said earlier that if you want money you can come to the church, and I'd find some work for you to do, and you can earn it. That offer still stands."

When the boy had left Loren turned to Olivia and motioned to the doorway, "Somehow Keyvon convinces me that we're where we should be. Whaddya' think? Let's start that school."

Olivia, resigned to what she assumed was inevitable, smiled and nodded.

So they did, but Loren never saw Keyvon again.

CHAPTER THREE

The bidding on the five "flowers" proceeded over the course of the next half hour. The children were paraded out in view of the buyers one at a time, and Luis elicited bids from each. It was hard to tell whether they were buying for themselves or for a client. No unnecessary words were exchanged between any of them.

Carlos managed to purchase two young girls while the others went to each of the other three bidders.

When the sale was concluded Carlos brought up the matter of the Anglo girl. "So, are we going to be bidding on the blond one or not, Luis?"

"I told you earlier, my friend, she's not for sale. In fact, she's no longer here. Now, I trust you gentlemen have had an enjoyable evening, and I wish you safe travels. Allow me to show you to the door."

Carlos was stunned, but he didn't show it. "Where *is* the girl?" he asked, trying to suppress any suggestion of urgency in his voice.

"I cannot discuss that with you, *señor*, but she's not here. She was shipped out this afternoon. A man to whom we have, ah, obligations apparently has tastes similar to those of your employer."

It was clear that nothing was to be gained from further inquiries so Carlos joined the other buyers who were ushering their purchases across the room toward the exit. Tattoo and Fat Man remained in the living room while Luis walked ahead to open the door. He was in high spirits, having netted approximately $80,000 this lovely afternoon.

As the group approached the door, they were startled to hear a sound like someone dropping a sack of flour on the front porch, followed quickly by another.

Luis reached for the door which suddenly flew open in his face, and three men dressed in sand-colored military garb swept into the living room with weapons pointed in Carlos' and Luis' faces. Two men took positions on either side of the doorway, their laser gunsights scanning the room for threats. The startled buyers instinctively threw their hands in the air, but Tattoo reached for the semiautomatic in the holster under his arm.

Two quick, muffled noises that sounded like *pfit, pfit* spat from the muzzle of one of the attacker's weapons, and Tattoo crumpled to the floor mortally wounded. Fat Man immediately thrust his hands over his head in a frantic signal of surrender.

A fourth person, a woman dressed in the same style as the men, now entered the room, gathered the children, and herded them out to Carlos' van while the men knocked out ceiling tiles, stood the buyers on pieces of furniture, and handcuffed them to the pipes running overhead. Luis and Carlos were blindfolded, cuffed, and shoved outside where they almost stumbled over the bodies of the two thugs who had frisked Carlos earlier. Luis, probing one of the bodies with his foot, realized that the thuds he'd heard a few minutes before were his employees dropping dead on the porch.

Back in the house, the raiders searched the building for additional children and more of Luis' henchmen. Finding none, they gathered up the satchels full of cash and probed the pockets of the handcuffed men for cell phones and car keys. When they exited the house, a mere six minutes after they'd entered it, they took Carlos' keys and one of the

men drove his van and the children away from the house. The female associate sat in the back with the children to offer them comfort after the trauma they'd endured over the last few days, culminating in the sudden violence they'd just witnessed.

Carlos and Luis were loaded rudely into a white Ford Explorer that had been driven to the *hacienda* by the Asian buyer. Carlos was pushed so hard that he struck his head on the car's door frame. Angered by the insult and the pain he launched a torrent of curses at his abductors who ignored him, slammed the door shut, and climbed in the front of the car. The stream of abuse continued from Carlos until one of the men turned and pushed the muzzle of his weapon against Carlos' forehead declaring that if Carlos didn't shut up he'd "relieve his pain for him right now." Carlos sullenly complied, and the Explorer followed the van out the dirt drive to the paved road.

One of the men in front spoke into a thin microphone attached to a headset: "Three bad guys down, two captured, four left cuffed to the plumbing. Five kids extracted. No sign of the Anglo girl."

After that the man who pointed the gun at Carlos, an ex-SEAL named Colin, began to ask both of his captives questions about the whereabouts of the missing girl. Carlos denied having any knowledge, and Luis refused to talk. After several minutes of fruitless interrogation Colin gave up. His prisoners were going to require more incentive than what he could offer them in the car. No one in the vehicle spoke again for the forty five minutes it took them to reach their destination on the outskirts of a small village twenty miles west of Cuidad Juarez.

It was 7:00 p.m. Caleb was standing in the living room with some friends who were on their way out after having dropped by with several covered dishes and lots of encouragement. As he opened the door for them he saw the same two men who'd been there earlier in the day coming up the walkway.

Caleb turned to alert his wife and, as his other visitors were leaving, invited the men into the house. He was so anxious to hear word of Alicia that he could scarcely wait until Patty joined him in the living room to ask them what news they brought. Having these men return put him in a state of unbearable suspense.

"I'm afraid we have some disappointing news," John said once Patty had emerged from the kitchen. "Alicia was not among the children we rescued today."

"Disappointing" did not begin to describe the feeling that hit Caleb and Patty like a punch to the stomach. Having allowed their hopes to rise earlier when they were told that Alicia had been located, they were devastated to learn that she'd not only *not* been rescued, but that her whereabouts were once again unknown. They both sank onto the sofa and covered their faces with their hands. Patty tried vainly to muffle her sobs out of consideration for her guests whom she needlessly feared might be embarrassed by her display of emotion.

But at least Alicia was still alive. For that they were thankful.

John softened the blow a little by revealing that the rescue team had captured someone who was likely to have knowledge of where Alicia might be. He was being questioned, and the information he provided would dictate the team's next move.

The grief-stricken couple clung to each other as John explained the general situation without disclosing details of the raid on the traffickers' house. It was all the Hoffmeyers could do to listen to him amidst their bitter disappointment.

John concluded that the team was hopeful that they'd be able to get the information they needed from the man they'd apprehended.

"But what if he doesn't tell you?" Patty asked in a voice quavering in near-panic.

"I think he'll tell us ma'am. Our guys are pretty good at persuading people to talk."

Caleb looked at the man incredulously. It was dawning on him that John was implying the unthinkable, and it horrified him. Caleb and Patty were pacifists who deplored the use of any kind of violence, including violence employed to coerce a confession, or, as in this case, life-saving information.

Caleb took a moment to collect himself and then asked, "Are you saying that you'll actually *torture* this man?"

"Torture's not a word we use, sir. We'll try to be very persuasive in convincing him that it's in his best interests to cooperate with us."

"But if that involves inflicting pain, if you're going to make him suffer, I don't think...we can't go along with that."

Michael, the taller African-American man who accompanied John, had remained silent throughout both visits to the Hoffmeyer home, but now he broke in somewhat impatiently. "Mr. Hoffmeyer," he said with his eyes boring in on Caleb's, "do you want us to do everything we can to get your daughter back?"

"Of course, but, I mean, not *that*. That's ... that's just evil."

"Well, we're not here to debate with you sir," Michael replied cooly, "but if that's what has to be done to get her back, are you saying you'd rather *not* have her back?"

That suggestion brought Caleb to the edge of anger, an emotion he rarely indulged. "No, of course that's not what I'm saying, but ...."

"We'll be in touch when we hear something," John quickly interjected, sensing that the atmosphere was getting tense, and with that the two men turned and left. Walking toward their car Michael said softly, "I wonder what they'd have said if they knew *everything* that happened today."

John grunted. "It's best they don't know. They have enough to worry about without burdening their consciences, too."

❦

A half hour after the visit by CSR Loren Holt stopped by to check on the Hoffmeyers one last time for the day. Willis and his wife arrived by coincidence about ten minutes later.

As the five took seats around the living room Caleb and Patty related the news their earlier visitors had brought and became visibly perturbed as they recounted the brief exchange concerning how CSR hoped to pry the information from the man they'd captured.

Willis was outraged at the revelation. He'd grown up in the same pacifist tradition as his brother, and although he had subsequently abandoned the religious underpinnings of the tradition, he still held fervently to the pacifism.

"What kind of men are these?" He demanded. "*Who* are they? Caleb, you really should contact the FBI. These guys sound like a bunch of reckless vigilantes taking the law into their own hands. They're going to wind up getting people killed."

"If they're torturing people," Marie added, "they have to be stopped."

Caleb slowly shook his head, his face revealing the pain that squeezed his heart like a vise. Rubbing his forehead with his fingertips, he half-mumbled, "I don't disagree with anything you're saying, but what if it's the only way to get Alicia back?" He raised his anguished eyes to meet those of his brother and sisiter-in-law, as if searching their faces for an answer. He was clearly conflicted between his love for his daughter and his desire not to be complicit in what he considered a moral horror.

"Doesn't the Bible say that you shouldn't do evil in order to achieve good?" Willis asked, turning toward Loren. His initial encounter with Caleb's pastor earlier that day failed to result in fond feelings for the clergyman, but he thought he'd be able to call on him for support on this matter, at least.

Before Loren could answer his first question, Willis asked him point blank whether he agreed that CSR had to be stopped from torturing the men they held in custody.

Loren sensed a prickly edge to the question. He stared for a few moments at a photograph of Caleb's parents on the far wall. A reply was coalescing in his mind, one he wanted very much to make because it tied in with their earlier conversation, but he wasn't sure that this was an appropriate time to make it. He was fairly sure that the last thing Caleb and Patty wanted or needed to hear was a debate. Even so, he spoke what was on his mind and hoped that it wouldn't offend.

"I'm not sure whether they should be stopped, Willis, but before I explain why, I'm puzzled by your reaction to what Caleb's told us. Why do you think it's wrong to use torture to rescue Alicia?"

Willis was taken aback by Holt's question, and sputtered his rejoinder. "It's wrong because it dehumanizes people, Reverend Holt. It's wrong to strip a man of his humanity."

After this remonstrance it dawned on Willis that Loren was pressing him on exactly the issue that had arisen between them earlier in the day. He was asking for the grounds upon which an atheist like Willis can declare anything, even torture, to be a moral evil.

"Please, call me Loren." Loren repeated the request he'd made that morning. "Yes, I think so, too, but you told me this morning that you're a Darwinian, Willis. Why, on Darwinian grounds, do you think it's wrong to dehumanize people?"

"Because human beings are intrinsically valuable, of course," Willis replied. "It's always wrong to violate someone's human dignity."

Loren nodded slightly but said nothing. It was obvious to Willis that Loren didn't think much of his answer.

"You don't agree with that, Pastor?"

"No, I don't, Willis. I'm wondering where intrinsic value comes from if human beings are just flesh and blood machines produced by accident by a blind natural process like evolution."

"Well, it just does!"

Willis realized that this was at best a feeble response born of frustration at not having more plausible answers with which to parry Holt's questions. He couldn't think of a better answer at the moment, and he was peeved that Holt was pushing him on the matter. That such things as torture were moral horrors he had never questioned, and to have someone insist he explain *why* he thought so, when everyone just *knew* that it was so, caught him very much off guard. He sought to salvage his position by maneuvering Holt into agreeing with him.

"Surely, as a Christian pastor, you don't dispute that, do you?"

"No, I don't, but only because I'm a theist, Willis. I believe God exists, but if I were an atheist and a Darwinian I'd have a very difficult time coming up with a reason why it'd be wrong to deprive someone of their humanity. I'd have a very difficult time, I think, explaining why cruelty is wrong when it seems to come so naturally to so many human beings.

"In any case we can talk about this another time. I don't think Caleb and Patty want to talk about it now." Loren shot a glance at the bereaved couple as he said this, half expecting them to be appalled that he would have initiated a disagreement with Willis at such an inopportune moment. He was surprised, therefore, at Caleb's reply.

"Actually, I do, Loren. I want to know what your opinion is about this. Both of us are really torn. We don't know what to think. It's easy to condemn violence until it becomes necessary, maybe, to save the life of your daughter, and then what's right isn't so certain anymore."

Loren caught a glimpse of Patty nodding her head in agreement. She was a very quiet woman, reserved to the point of shyness, who usually preferred to listen to others rather than voice her own views. On this question, she was anxious to hear what her pastor would say.

"Well," Loren began after a respectful pause. "I just know that were I in your place, and I got my daughter back because her rescuers had inflicted pain on her abductors, I couldn't imagine looking her in the eyes and telling her that I love her very much, and I'm so happy that she's back and safe, but that I'd rather she not have been saved from the men who kidnapped her, and possibly beat and molested her, if it meant that those men be hurt in order to accomplish her rescue.

I mean, that's essentially what you'd be saying to her, isn't it?" He looked at Willis as he posed the question.

Willis wasn't sure he wanted to answer what he saw as a loaded question so he asked a question of his own.

"Are you saying that the ends justify the means, Pastor? Some things are just absolutely wrong regardless of the consequences." He added the assertion before Loren had a chance to respond to his question.

"But Willis, if there's no God how can anything be absolutely wrong? How can anything even be *wrong* at all? It's like I was saying this afternoon, the most we can say, if we think there's no God, is that there are some things people do that we find distasteful, we wish they wouldn't do them, but that doesn't make them *wrong*. If you think there are absolute wrongs, and I agree with you that there are, you should jettison your atheism and become a Christian, or at least a theist."

Loren wasn't sure he was capable himself of doing anything like what Caleb was afraid CSR was doing to their prisoner, but he was pretty sure he couldn't condemn those who did if that was what was necessary to save a little girl from the horror of sex slavery. He was also pretty sure that an atheist like Willis had no grounds for condemning anyone for doing anything.

"Torture is certainly wrong almost always, Willis, but I just can't say that if it's the only way to get Alicia back it'd be wrong to use it. Things that are morally horrible are not always morally wrong. Let's just pray that they don't have to use it."

"That doesn't sound very Christian to me, I must say, Pastor," Willis responded with a trace of acerbity in his voice.

"Well, I hope that it's not *un*christian, Willis. Christians are called to love others and to do justice. The difficulty we have living in a fallen world is in deciding who, in a situation like this, has the strongest claim on our love and justice. Is it Alicia or the men who've kidnapped her? It's hard in this case to see how it can be both. Love and justice each sometimes means being willing to do what you personally abhor to protect the innocent, especially when that innocent person is someone who has been entrusted into your care by God.

"The problem with life," he added by way of conclusion, "is that the more we live it, the more we experience it, the more it upsets our tidy little dogmas."

Loren and Willis both noticed that Patty had covered her face with her hands and was weeping quietly. Not only was she distraught over her daughter, but she was overcome with self-recrimination for having let Alicia walk to the party alone instead of driving her there herself.

With a reproachful glance cast at Loren, whom she obviously blamed for Patty's disquiet, Marie rose from her chair and gently led Patty into the kitchen.

Despite Caleb's assurances to the contrary, both men felt badly that their exchange had apparently upset his wife.

"Maybe we should put this off 'til another time," Loren said quietly.

Willis nodded in agreement, and both rose to leave.

As Willis and Marie stood on the front step in the light of a pair of porch lamps, having promised that they'd be back next day, Willis turned to Loren and repeated what he'd said that morning. He felt he had to say this one more thing, and he voiced the thought politely, even kindly.

"Pastor, the world has been modernized, secularized, disenchanted. There's no going back. You're living in a world that no longer exists."

Loren smiled. "Maybe so, Willis, but modern, secular man, for all his protests to the contrary, is still religious. He still searches for meaning, he still makes moral judgments, he still yearns for justice, but he tries to do all this while denying the only thing that can make any of it possible. Instead of a transcendent ground for these yearnings he substitutes music, art, literature, drugs, sex, consumerism, sports, moral fashion, political correctness–whatever he thinks will give him a reason to believe that meaning and the rest are possible. But still he senses, when he stops to think about it, that something's missing, that he's left out something important, something necessary. What's missing is the God he refuses to accept."

Loren smiled again, turned and began walking to his car parked a half block away, leaving Willis and Marie standing on the step, staring at Holt as he walked off into the dark November night.

On their way home Marie could tell that her husband's mind was churning.

"What are you thinking, Willis?"

Her husband let out a long, weary sigh. "I was just thinking that I don't know why I keep talking to him. I tell myself I'm not accomplishing anything, it's not doing any good, he's not going to listen, he's not going to change his mind, but it's as if I can't help myself. I keep telling myself to 'let it go,' but for some reason I don't."

As they made their way along I-695 around the city Willis reflected on his encounters that day with Loren Holt. It was true that there were times when visiting an art museum or an old cathedral or listening to Bach or Handel he felt … something. Perhaps it was a sense that the art had a depth and richness about it, a power to move the soul, because the men who created it were expressing a deep belief through it. The men who toiled to create beautiful architecture, or painting, or music were trying to communicate a deeply felt Truth about the way the world was. Strip away that Truth, deny the meaning the artists invested in their art, and it all seemed ordinary, or at least less impressive, less moving. The artist might be admired for his skill, but when the meaning of what he created is ignored, so much of its beauty and power seemed lost.

He had to admit, reluctantly, that Holt had a point. Literature and art and the rest of those things to which moderns resort to give their lives meaning once they decide they can no longer believe in God turn out to be pretty insubstantial, almost sterile. Something is missing, Willis conceded. Something crucially important is being left out.

He laughed to himself as he recalled a quip by the writer Julian Barnes: "I don't believe in God, but I miss him." That thought seemed to capture perfectly what Willis was feeling at the moment.

He turned to Marie and smiled. "That preacher's an interesting guy. Very wrong, but interesting even so."

The team leader, a short, muscular man named Sam Williams, awaited the CSR team at their safe-house several kilometers west of Cuidad Juarez. As soon as the group arrived Luis and Carlos were shoved down a stairway to a cement-floor basement where their blindfolds were removed. They found themselves in a room in the center of which stood a steel pole supporting the floor above.

Luis glimpsed a box of tools on a table near the pole. At first he thought nothing of it, but then icy tendrils of terror began creeping down his spine into his legs when he realized what they were for. Even more terrifying was a chain saw resting on the floor near the pole. He felt himself getting sick to his stomach and the muscles in his legs began to fail him. His mouth parched, as though filled suddenly with dry sand, and sweat beaded profusely on his forehead as the reality of what was in store for him began to sink in.

Carlos was stripped naked and placed with his back to the pole. His hands were freed, then yanked roughly around the column, and refastened behind him. Meanwhile, Luis was taken through a door to an adjacent room where he was subjected to the same procedure. The rooms were separated by a cinderblock wall. The only way out of the basement was by way of the stairs.

Having secured their prisoners, the team met briefly upstairs to assess the raid and plan their next move. They weren't happy with the way things had played out that afternoon.

They'd made dozens of rescues in the six or seven years they'd been engaged in the work, but rarely was violence needed and never as much violence as was employed on this occasion. Most of the team was troubled by it. They agreed that, given the plan that they'd decided to execute, the bloodshed was almost inevitable. They also agreed that the three casualties were no loss to humanity. They were murderous drug thugs and human traffickers of the worst sort, selling children to be used as playthings by wealthy pedophiles. They agreed on all that, but they still didn't like it. Nor did they like the fact that the children they rescued today, and who were presently being cared for in another room, were put in serious danger of being caught in a crossfire.

Moreover, they feared that corpses would draw the notice of the Mexican police, and maybe–once those left back at the *hacienda* tell the authorities that it appeared that at least some of the killers were Americans–the notice of their own government in Washington as well.

Finally, they were very uncomfortable working without any legal authority. Although they understood why this was necessary–they understood that legalities would either hamstring them or altogether prevent them from rescuing these children–it didn't make them feel much better about what they were doing.

They certainly weren't the only group that sought to rescue children from people like Luis, but other organizations regarded CSR, to the extent they were even aware of them, as a fringe outfit because of their willingness to use force and work outside the laws of the countries they operated in. Some even wanted them disbanded.

Nevertheless, they didn't have time to ponder their misgivings. There were a number of tasks that required immediate attention.

It turned out that of the five children they'd rescued two were Americans, both apparently from Los Angeles. The others were from villages in northern Mexico and would have to be handed over surreptitiously to the Mexican authorities. The American children would be returned to the states and reunited with their families, but all these transfers would have to be done without exposing themselves to the police or border patrol.

They'd also soon have to contact the local police and inform them, anonymously, of the men trussed up back at the *hacienda*. They didn't wish to leave those men like that for more than a couple of hours, but they needed to be well away from the area when they were found.

And they had to interrogate their prisoners. They had been instructed by their chief in Washington to find out where the Anglo girl–by now they'd learned her name was Alicia–had been taken.

After about a ten minute interval designed to give the pair downstairs time to contemplate the seriousness of their predicament, several of the team returned to the basement. One of them entered the room where Luis was braced against the steel pole.

El Jefe watched with rapidly growing horror as this man opened a satchel and took out what looked like a taser, a soldering iron, a pliers, and some kind of drill. He laid these on a table which he pushed close to Luis. Luis could feel his blood turning to ice water. His naked body sagged limply against the pole.

Suddenly Carlos' panicked voice could be heard from the other side of the block wall begging not to be tortured. He insisted he knew nothing, that he was just a buyer. His pleas were growing increasingly desperate. Then an ear-piercing scream, followed by another, filled the entire house.

"Who are you people?" Luis shouted angrily at the man who stood before him pulling on latex gloves. The man looked at Luis impassively and said nothing.

"What do you want from me?" Sweat was dripping from his forehead. Carlos could be heard screaming, whimpering, and begging for them to stop whatever it was they were doing to him. One man could be heard telling another to gag him so that he didn't make so much noise. Then Luis' eyes bulged in horror and his face turned pallid when someone in the next room pulled the starter cord on the chain saw.

"What do I want from you?" The man finally acknowledged Luis' question. "What I want from you is where that Anglo girl was taken. I want a name and an address. If I get it then maybe the people upstairs will let you live. If I don't then…" His voiced trailed off as he nodded in the direction of Carlos who had suddenly gone quiet.

"But I don't know nothing. I don't know where the girl is," Luis protested.

"Yeah, that's what your *amigo* over there's been saying, too," and the man made a face as if to say that it's not working out so well for him.

Luis was now trembling with fear. His mouth was completely dry, he had already lost control of his bowels once, and his knees had turned to rubber. He was sure they'd soon give out. He could feel vomit welling up in his throat. The man was rubbing gel on Luis' bare abdomen and toying with the taser. How much pain could he withstand, and for what should he try to endure it? To protect some *pervertido* higher up in the cartel hierarchy than he was? The drug smuggler who was going to wind up with the girl was going to be arrested or gunned down sooner or later anyway. It happened to all of them eventually. The Mexican military and the American DEA were working more closely than ever to make arrests, and rival cartels were merrily extirpating each other with ruthless and macabre efficiency. Headless torsos were turning up with alarming regularity across the Mexican countryside, and thousands of cartel foot soldiers and higher-ups had reached their expiration date over the last decade.

Luis was growing increasingly desperate. "Maybe," he reasoned to himself, "if I tell these people what they're asking me for no one will ever know where the information came from." He was rapidly approaching all-out panic. He could think only of the chainsaw and what it would do to him. Ten years ago he'd witnessed a man dismembered in precisely that fashion for having turned informant for the police, and he almost passed out as he watched it. The scene haunted his dreams even to this day.

"Look, if I give you what you want to know, what happens to me? Will you give me your word that you'll let me go?" Luis could force the question out of his uncooperative lips and tongue only slowly and with great effort. His mouth was so desiccated he had trouble forming words, the muscles shaping them seemed paralyzed. His legs had no strength left. Had he not been strapped to the post he'd surely have collapsed. His whole body was shaking. Tears streamed down his cheeks.

"Can't do that. You give me the name and address, and you'll be treated better than you deserve while we check it. If it all checks out then you live. Maybe we hand you over to the local *policia*."

That gave Luis hope. It was exactly what he wanted. He knew the municipal police would give him little more than a slap on the wrist and let him go. Many of them, after all, were on his payroll, and the ones who weren't really had nothing much on him in any case.

"*Sí, sí. Por favor. Un momento. Agua.*"

After a brief respite to pull himself together Luis began answering the questions CSR put to him, and even some they didn't. Upstairs the rest of the team was sitting around the room quietly listening to the interrogation on a speaker. The entire proceedings in the basement were being recorded.

At length the men listening in heard the basement door open. As they turned to look a pony-tailed man emerged grinning and buttoning his shirt.

"Did it work?" he whispered.

"He's singing like an opera diva, Carlos," Sam Williams replied with a smile.

CHAPTER FOUR

T he hour was late so Caleb Hoffmeyer was startled by the buzz of his cell phone telling him he had a call. A glance at the screen told him it was from Michael. A cold shiver of anxiety rushed up the middle of his back and spread across his shoulders. He closed his eyes and said a quick prayer before answering.

"It's Michael," he shouted to Patty who was in another room. He put the phone on speaker and said hello.

"Hello, Caleb. I just called to tell you that we were able to get a lead on where Alicia might be. We have a team on its way there now."

Patty squeezed Caleb's hand tightly.

"Can you tell us anything about what's going on?" Caleb knew that Michael's partner John was pretty tight-lipped, but he hoped that maybe Michael might be more willing to offer some details.

Michael was silent for a moment. At length he said, "Not over the phone. If you'd like I can stop by tomorrow morning. I have a favor I want to ask of you anyway."

"That'd be fine. We'll both be here," Caleb agreed. "Neither of us can even think about going to work until we get Alicia back." Nor could he imagine what Michael's favor could be.

The interrogation of Luis had continued into the night. A voice could be heard through the cinder block wall saying matter-of-factly that Carlos was passed out and was dying from shock and loss of blood. Luis couldn't hear all of it, nor did he care to. All he cared about, all he had ever cared about, for that matter, was himself and his own well-being.

"I want the people who took the girl," the interrogator quietly insisted. "How many there were, what they were driving, where they were going, their route, and what time they picked her up."

Through the wall Luis could hear one man tell the other to dump the body out back and hose down the floor. A couple of moments later water started seeping through gaps at the base of the wall and flowed past Luis' bare feet toward the drain a meter in front of him. It was blood red.

With one eye on the instruments on the table, and the sound of the chain saw and Carlos' screams still ringing in his ears, Luis divulged all of the information his interrogator demanded. It was then that the team texted Michael, precipitating his call to Caleb Hoffmeyer.

As Luis talked he managed to calm down enough to bring his shaking under control.

"Look, you're not *policia* and you're not Zeta or Sinaloa," a reference to two notorious and very violent Mexican drug cartels. "I've given you everything you wanted. You're an honorable man. Give me a guarantee that I'll be let go, and I'll give you something you didn't ask for."

"No promises, but if it's good, I'm sure that'll be taken into account."

Luis figured that that was about the best he could hope for. "One of the men who picked up the Anglo girl said they were going to stop for the night at a *posada* in Cumpas."

The interrogator nodded, knowing the information was being noted upstairs, and continued to probe for the names of the connections in Los Angeles and Baltimore who had provided the children to Luis. He also wanted to know how the children were brought across the border. Luis couldn't, or wouldn't, provide too many specifics, but he revealed that in the past girls had been flown in a private jet to Arizona and then smuggled across the border via underground tunnels. He didn't know where the tunnels were, but they were used by the cartels for drug smuggling as well as human trafficking. He also divulged the name of a man in Baltimore that sometimes came up in conversation.

More than that he professed himself unable to say, nor was he sure about who the people were in Los Angeles who had abducted the children there, but he happily offered the name of the man in Baltimore to the gentleman with the latex gloves and sundry scalpels, drills, and saws, all of which were props in a well-rehearsed charade.

"I have one more question for you, Luis. Did the people in Baltimore ever send you a black girl, like about two years ago?"

Luis thought for a moment. "No, I don't remember any black girls."

The fear he felt during the raid, seeing men he knew shot and killed, and now the terror he had just experienced at the thought of being tortured by this man was taking its toll on Luis' nerves. He was about to collapse in exhaustion from his ordeal.

⁖

The information Luis had provided was encouraging. Two men in the employ of an up-and-coming drug smuggler and human trafficker named Felix Castro had taken possession of the girl about 3:00 that afternoon. They were driving a white Honda SUV and planned to stop at a hotel along highway 17 near or in the town of Cumpas on their way to Castro's ranch near Empalme along the coast of the Gulf of California. Cumpas was about a five hour drive from the safe house.

It was now almost 10:00 p.m. If they left soon they could be there by 3:00 in the morning.

Three men, Carlos, Colin, and another member of the team named Tyrone, quickly gathered their gear and prepared for the long drive down a lonely Mexican highway, hoping that the information provided by Luis was correct. They were thoroughly fatigued from all that had transpired that day, but they worried that if they didn't leave immediately Alicia would be gone, possibly forever.

The remainder of the CSR team stayed behind with the rescued children and Luis, who was certain that his future, if there were to be one, depended on the accuracy of what he'd revealed to his interrogator.

Somebody in the group had had the foresight to stash a couple of five gallon containers of gasoline in a shed behind the safe house. They were sure to need fuel at some point, and it wasn't likely that there'd be many gas stations along their route, especially stations that were open at this hour.

The team made their way west in the SUV they'd purloined from the Asian buyer earlier that evening. Their route took them along a lonely two lane highway partially illuminated by a nearly full moon suspended in a clear night sky.

While Tyrone drove, Colin busied himself hollowing out a portion of the rear seat, fashioning a place to conceal their weapons in case they were stopped by police.

Each man retreated into his own thoughts, lulled by the quiet purr of the Explorer's engine and the thrumming of its tires churning along the highway.

Each man in the team was a combat veteran. Each had come to CSR by a different path. Two of the men were "contractors." They had families and regular jobs, but were available to the organization whenever they're skills were needed. The rest, including Carlos, worked pretty much full-time for CSR.

They were supported by gifts from donors who admired them and the work they did, although few outside their immediate circle knew much more than the vaguest of details. They also, of course, supported themselves by confiscating cash like the $80,000 they'd managed to heist from Luis during their earlier raid on the *hacienda*.

Carlos closed his eyes. He was exhausted and wanted to get a little sleep on the way, but his adrenaline kept him wide awake. His mind went back to the horrible event that ultimately got him involved with CSR.

His older brother, whom he deeply admired, his brother's wife, and their 14 year-old daughter were camping in Big Bend National Park in Texas ten years before. The campground was otherwise deserted. They were sitting around a campfire when three men appeared out of the darkness with guns. They held Carlos' brother at gunpoint while they raped his wife and daughter in front of him. When his brother tried to stop them they shot him dead. When they were done they shot his wife and daughter, too, and left them all for dead. The family was discovered by Park rangers the next day.

Somehow Carlos' niece had survived this nightmare to tell what had happened. Her body eventually healed, but her soul was permanently scarred. She made progress in therapy, but it was a long slow road to recovery, and Carlos knew she'd never be the same outgoing, fun-loving young woman she was before that night.

They were a family of Catholic missionaries who had devoted their lives to doing God's work among the poor. Carlos wondered how the God they served could have let people who loved him, who devoted themselves to him, suffer so horribly.

One of the men was eventually caught and under questioning confessed that he was part of a sex trafficking ring that had been smuggling people both ways across the border to work as prostitutes. They were going to take Carlos' niece, but she was so badly beaten they thought she was dead. They put a bullet in her to make sure before they fled. That she had survived seemed a miracle.

Carlos was so emotionally undone by this unspeakable crime, and the devastation and pain it wrought in his parents' lives, that he cast about for some way to do something to wipe the scourge of such men from the world. He heard about CSR through a friend and was put in contact with John in Washington. Carlos was an ex-special-ops veteran of Iraq, but he was also a talented actor. He was well-suited for the role he'd played yesterday.

When he first joined the team he wanted revenge. He wanted to kill every trafficker he encountered, at least those trafficking in kidnapped children, but the words of a priest from his boyhood kept echoing in his mind. The priest was a man whom Carlos deeply loved and respected. He was perhaps the saintliest man Carlos had ever known, and for a time he thought he wanted to become a priest himself so he could be like this man.

The priest had told him once that, "The world is full of bad men. What it needs is more good ones. You be one of the good ones, Carlos."

Those simple words stuck with him and constrained him throughout his life to act in ways he thought that priest would approve. At one point he was close to going to seminary, but he joined the military instead, and that decision put his life on a much different path.

But the tension of these missions was wearing him down, and not only him, but all of them. They had not only to be concerned about being shot by some thug, they also had to be wary of both the Mexican police–who would have thrown them into a prison from which they'd probably never emerge if they were caught–and the American authorities who would doubtless be only slightly less forgiving. They also feared for the safety of the children if a mission went badly. And now they were cruising down a barren Mexican highway, trying to suppress their anxiety over the prospect of encountering a checkpoint manned by Mexican military. Their weapons were stowed out of sight, they all had passports, but one could never tell when something might suddenly go wrong. It seemed like just a matter of time until their luck ran out and they were apprehended, or worse. It played on all their nerves, though none of them allowed it to show.

Carlos had talked about it with Erin, the female member of the team who had shepherded the children. She'd flown helicopters in the army, and then went into military intelligence work. After her discharge from the service she heard about human trafficking in her church and felt strongly that she should and could contribute to the fight against it.

She was valuable to the team because many of the children they rescued had been traumatized by men to the point that the CSR males often terrified the children simply by their proximity. It was much better to have a woman handle the children in the immediate aftermath of a rescue.

She got her start with CSR working amongst prostitutes in Miami and elsewhere. She tried to develop relationships with them and discover which ones had been trapped into the trade, which ones wanted to escape, and assist those who wished to get out.

Eventually, the handlers and pimps of these women realized what she was doing, and one night she found herself staring into the muzzle of a gun as a pimp threatened to "blow her brains out" if he ever saw her on his street talking to his girls again.

This close encounter with death didn't deter Erin, but she started carrying a weapon of her own after that.

That's how it seemed to start for all of them. At first they rescued girls by stealth and trickery, but the men who were invested in these women were often violent sociopaths. For their own protection CSR personnel started carrying weapons, but once armed they felt more confident in taking on more dangerous operations. Those operations, in turn, sometimes necessitated the use of their weapons, and the use of force led on occasions like the present one to the practice of interrogating sources, and that led to the sort of staged theatrics they had employed earlier that night.

Erin had expressed concern about the direction the rescues were headed, but saving those children was such a high priority for her, every incremental increase of violence in their methodology seemed easy to justify. It was the overall pattern that troubled her, and troubled Carlos, too.

Carlos had no doubt that had the fakery not worked on Luis someone on the team would have been prepared to carry out the real thing on him, and that alarmed him. He felt the team was descending into a pit of violence that was deeply disturbing. The worst part was he had no doubt that were he convinced that Luis had information on this girl they were pursuing he would have assented to whatever means it took to get it out of him.

Colin and Tyrone were both part-timers. Colin was an ex-Marine sniper who served tours in Africa and Yemen and had trouble adjusting to civilian life. For him CSR provided an adrenalin rush that he couldn't find anywhere else outside the military. Like all of them, he was committed to the cause of rescuing children, and was profoundly gratified when a child was successfully reunited with grieving parents, but he found the danger of the missions psychologically therapeutic as well. Carlos suspected that Colin was not as concerned about the growing body count as he was.

Beyond the fact that he was a vet, Carlos didn't know much about Tyrone, or how he came to be involved with CSR. He knew that Ty was related somehow to Michael and assumed that Michael had recruited him into the organization.

For the next five hours the men would take turns driving and sleeping and wondering what, if anything, they would find in Cumpas.

Luis had been released from the pole, allowed to dress, and strapped into a chair. His feet were shackled and his hands immobilized behind him.

The man who had interrogated him–his name was Danny Howe, 32 years old and, like his fellow CSR operatives, a military veteran–brought some bottled water which he held for Luis to drink. Having slaked his thirst Luis watched as Danny placed a bowl of *pollo y arroz* on his lap, freed one of his hands, and sat down in a chair across from him. Danny drank from a thermos of hot coffee to keep himself awake while Luis ate greedily with his free hand. Danny was amazed that despite the stress Luis had just endured, despite what he certainly thought had been done to Carlos, he still had an appetite.

His mouth full of chicken, Luis managed to mumble a question. "What happened to ...?" He completed the sentence by waving a chicken wing in the direction of the cinderblock wall behind which Carlos had been held.

"He didn't talk so he didn't make it," Danny answered matter-of-factly.

Luis grunted. "He didn't talk because he didn't *know* anything," he replied with a thick dollop of sarcasm, his mouth still full. "He was just a buyer."

"Too bad," Danny replied curtly. "He should've gone into a different line of work."

"I said you were an honorable man, *señor*, but you're also hard. *Muy* cruel."

"Yeah, well, that's the world we live in."

Luis was silent for a moment. "Tell me, *mi amigo*, do you believe in God?" He asked the question while licking his fingers.

The query seemed to come out of the blue, but it brought to mind thoughts Danny had been having intermittently since the raid earlier that evening. Danny was the man who had shot Tattoo, although Luis didn't know that, and when he wasn't busy with Luis he'd been mentally replaying the raid over and over.

The assault team, Colin, Ty, Erin, and himself, had been concealed in the van when Carlos drove up to the *hacienda*. During his earlier visit that morning Carlos had managed to plant a listening device in the living room which enabled the team to monitor what was going on during the "auction."

The original plan was for Carlos to purchase as many of the children as possible with Alicia being a priority. As many others as possible would be seized from the buyers later on the road to Cuidad Juarez. This would minimize violence and risk to everyone, but when the team in the van heard that Alicia was no longer in the house they realized that they had to take Luis in order to find out where she was, and they assumed they'd

have to scare him almost to death in order to get him to talk. Carlos was as surprised as anyone when his team burst through the door, but he quickly realized why the plan had changed and played along.

As the sale of the children was concluding, the men quietly opened the rear doors of the van and each of Danny's two teammates shot the guards on the porch before the victims realized what was happening. The three then ran to the porch just as Luis reached to open the door.

Luis was understandably startled to have the door fling open and to have the muzzle of a gun thrust in his face. Danny swept into the house first, followed by the others. The entire sequence of events seemed to transpire in slow motion. He recalled first seeing Carlos, and then Luis' astonished expression. Then his eyes caught the widening eyes of the buyers, and registered only for an instant the expressionless faces of the children, still in shock from the brutality of their abuse. His gaze swept past the children and fell on Fat Man, frozen in stunned disbelief, then Tattoo, the only man in the room not paralyzed by surprise, reaching to his shoulder holster for his 9 mm semi-automatic.

Danny reacted instinctively. The whole thing took maybe fifteen seconds, but it seemed much longer, and once it was over, once the adrenaline began to subside, he began to feel a deep disquiet. The questions and doubts began tumbling into his conscience. Was there another way? Could I have disabled the man without killing him? What kind of man am I? Do I have the right to play God?

He reminded himself that *somebody* has to do what he was doing. Those kids depended on it. He remembered hearing in the military an officer quote some famous person or other that all that's needed for evil to prevail in the world is for good men to do nothing, and he agreed that good men had to stand up to evil men, but when good men start killing evil men do the good men become what they're trying to eradicate? He believed it may sometimes be necessary to do awful things, but he also believed that if he ever found himself enjoying doing them then it was time to get out.

He had learned by experience in the military that seeing men die changes a man, especially if one is himself responsible for the deaths. It hardens him or it breaks him, but one way or the other he's never the same. At the least it makes him more distant, more walled off and isolated from those around him who've never taken a life and who could never understand. It's as if something in his soul withers and dies. Danny wondered how much of his own soul he'd lost over the last few years.

He also wondered whether he could have actually gone through with torturing Luis if Luis hadn't divulged the information on Alicia's whereabouts. Would he have been justified in doing whatever was necessary to rescue her even if that meant inflicting serious, crippling pain on one of the men responsible for her predicament? He asked himself again if he had the right to play God.

The question segued into wondering whether he even *believed* in God. He was pretty sure he stopped believing around the time he was a senior in high school as he watched his mother waste away and eventually die from cancer. Losing his mother like that caused him to doubt that there was a benevolent force behind the universe, and nothing that had happened in his life since then had given him any reason to change his mind. Now Luis was uncannily posing the very question to him he had been raising to himself, as though it were being held in front of him deliberately to force him to confront it.

Luis was eyeing him quizzically while awaiting an answer to his question whether Danny believed in God.

Danny closed his eyes briefly and gave a very slight shake of the head. "No."

"Then we are the same, you and I, no?"

"I'm nothing like you," was Danny's indignant reply.

"Oh, *sí*. We're both capable of cruelty, and why not? We both have the heart of beasts with a thin layer of civilization covering the brutishness." Here Luis used the thumb and index finger of his free hand to indicate the thinness. "Mother Nature has made us violent and heartless. Although," he added parenthetically, "you believe in honor. God only knows why. What does it matter when we die whether we were honorable or not, eh? When we die there's nothing more. The honorable man and the man without honor both have the same destiny, the same fate. It's all the same in the grave, *¿no lo es?* Is it not?"

"When you die, you're going to hell," Danny informed him.

"Correction, my friend," Luis held up his index finger. "If there's no God, there is no hell. But if there *is* a hell then we're both going there. *Tú y yo*. Me and you. Together. *Somos los mismos*. We're the same."

"I don't understand how you think."

"No? What's so hard?"

Danny ignored the question and changed the subject. "I hope for their sakes the people who took that girl didn't hurt her. Some of the guys on the team wouldn't take that well."

"I doubt they will," Luis assured him. "Castro made it very plain that the girl was not to be violated. He wanted that pleasure for himself, I presume."

"Sick dude."

Luis shrugged. "There are such men in the world. Probably a lot more than most people think. I've known others. Who's to say they're 'sick,' as you put it? They just consider children to be our most precious resource." He chuckled at this remark, evidently thinking it funny.

"Why do you say that's wrong, eh? Who are we that we should tell another man that he's sick?" Luis used the plural because it was less accusatory and less likely to anger his young interlocutor.

His words produced a fleeting doubt in Danny's mind, which was quickly supplanted by a feeling of disgust, a revulsion at the repugnant way Luis made his living.

"Don't you feel any remorse for what you do? Buying and selling human beings, little kids?"

"Remorse?!" Luis exclaimed. "You talk of remorse?! You and your friends kill three of my associates tonight, then butcher a man over there," with this he waved with some emphasis another piece of chicken in the direction of the other room, "and you ask me if *I* feel remorse? *Señor*, someone who cuts off men's limbs with chainsaws should not be lecturing others on remorse."

Luis paused momentarily to compose himself.

"Look, *amigo,* some men trade in goats, some in cattle, some in pigs. I traffic in humans. What's the difference, eh? Just a different kind of animal." Luis was gesticulating with his unshackled hand. "What makes one trade any better or worse than the other? We're all animals, are we not? We all come from the sea, do we not? Darwin, eh?"

"No. I'm not an animal."

"But, you told me you don't believe in God. How can you say you're not an animal? I don't think you've thought things through very much. Look, here's the difference between you and me, the *only* difference: You chase what you think is justice. *La niña*, the little girl, eh? I chase power, wealth and pleasure. Tell me what makes your pursuit better than mine? Why is yours right and mine wrong? Can you tell me?"

Danny had no answer. He thought there had to be one, it was so obvious to him that there was no moral comparison between what Luis was doing and what he himself was doing, but he realized when he was challenged to explain what that difference was he couldn't do it. Nor was he sure why his unbelief in God made any difference, but Luis apparently thought it did.

"Listen, *mi amigo,* here is the truth. We only live once. Why should we not just live for ourselves? Why should we deny our own pleasures so that others can be happy? Why is it wrong to care only for oneself? What does it even mean to say that it's wrong to live for one's own pleasure and satisfaction, if when we die we just disappear?"

"That sounds pretty selfish."

"*Sí*, but what's wrong with being selfish? You see, you judge me and say that I'm a bad man, but you cannot say *why* I'm bad. I'm not worse than you, I'm just more consistent, *coherente*, eh? Life is just a bad joke played on us by nature, is it not so? We're born, we suffer, we die, we're forgotten. What could it all mean? Nothing, *nada*. We might as well enjoy the life we have if we can."

Danny realized that he was out of his depth in this discussion. He'd never even thought about the questions Luis was asking let alone come up with answers to them. Rather than try to respond he just sat silently and let Luis talk.

Luis sat back in his chair with a smug expression on his face. He may still be in a precarious position and at this *gringo's* mercy, but it gave him satisfaction nonetheless to stymie him.

It was 3:17 in the morning when the Ford Explorer containing the three-man team from CSR rolled into the dusty town of Cumpas. They cruised slowly down the main street looking for the *posada* where Luis told them they'd find the two men and the girl. The town wasn't very big, but if the hotel was outside of town it may take a while to find it. On the off chance that it'd show up on the internet one of the men had googled it on his phone, but nothing came up. Nor did the satellite view of the town on Google Earth show much.

They made one pass through town and decided to check some side streets when Tyrone spotted a white Honda SUV parked outside an open-air *cantina* surrounded by a half dozen dilapidated cabins fifty yards down the first side street they tried.

Odd, they thought, Castro's drug smuggling business must not be going well if his employees are staying in this half-star establishment, but then this may well have been the only place for miles around where they could find any accommodations at all.

They pulled in behind the *cantina* to discuss how they should manage the takedown. The lights were off in the room and the curtains were pulled. Presumably the door was locked. Trying to break in would be too risky. They decided to wait until the girl's captors emerged from the room later in the morning. Meanwhile, they'd sleep in shifts.

The plan was for Erin, the female member of the team, to get the American kids back to Los Angeles by taking them to the American consulate in Cuidad Juarez that morning. In order to avoid awkward inquiries about her identity and how she came to be in possession of these children she googled a Catholic church in the city and located the rectory. She knocked on the door and explained in Spanish to the priest who answered that these children were Americans who needed to be taken to the consulate. She also explained that it wouldn't do for her to be the one to take them, and she requested that the priest be so good as to see that the children were handed over to the proper authorities.

The priest was a bit dumbfounded by all this, especially Erin's refusal to explain how the children came to be in her custody, but he eventually agreed. He called a cab and Erin followed them to the consulate to insure that the girls were safely delivered.

The other three children were to be taken to a local hospital with an envelope containing information on their identities, what had happened to them, and the villages from which they were originally kidnapped. They would be dropped off a short walk from the front door of the hospital, and Erin would wait to make sure they were safely inside before returning to the safe house.

CHAPTER FIVE

A t 9:00 that morning Michael stood on the front stoop of the Hoffmeyer's house and rang the doorbell. His partner, John, was back in their Washington, D.C. office, tending to CSR business.

Michael had hoped to have received word by now from the team in Mexico, but the only message they'd sent was a text giving the name of a man in Baltimore who may have been implicated in Alicia's abduction. The man's name was Enrico Gardonez. Michael had checked him out, but couldn't find an address or even a cell phone number. He decided he'd feed the name surreptitiously to the FBI and let them work it. They had a lot more resources than he did.

Patty answered the bell and invited Michael to take a chair in the living room while she went to fetch some tea. Caleb came out from a bedroom and took a seat on the sofa. Both of them were anxious for word about Alicia and hopeful that Michael was bearing better news than he had on his visit the previous day. The fact that he didn't tell them anything immediately gave them the sinking feeling that he either had no news or bad news.

The haggard parents were exhausted from worry and lack of sleep, but they did their best to make Michael feel welcome. When

Patty returned with the tea she sat down next to Caleb on the sofa and took his hand in hers.

Michael told them that he knew they were expecting word on Alicia, and he was sorry he didn't have anything new to report to them, but he was quite sure he'd hear something today from the team in Mexico. He waited politely and silently for a minute or so to allow the Hoffmeyers to adjust to this latest blow to their hopes and then proceeded on a different topic.

"I said last night that I had a favor to ask of you," he began. "I was wondering if you could tell me whatever you told the police and FBI about Alicia's kidnapping."

Michael's reasons for asking this were completely personal. Capital Search and Rescue didn't do police work, and they weren't investigating the kidnapping at this end. Their mission was simply to locate children sold into sex slavery, get them out, and, if they could, put the traffickers in prison.

Caleb thought the question a bit odd and asked Michael why he wanted them to go through this all over again. Michael was leaning forward in his chair with his elbows on his knees, hands clasped around his tea cup. He stared for a few moments at the beige carpet wondering if he should explain himself. He had a great deal of sympathy for the Hoffmeyer's and thought that if he told them his story it might do some good, at least for himself, if not also for them.

He exhaled deeply and began. "I had a little girl of my own. When she was five–that would've been about twelve years ago–I was assigned to counter-terrorism–I was in the military–I was sent to Africa to work on what was euphemistically called 'terror-suppression'. I don't want to get into the details of what that involved, but the mission required me to be there for long stretches of time. I only got home a few times a year. I loved my wife and little girl, and missed them a lot. Social media helped, when that became available, but doing what I was doing was no way to be a family."

Michael paused and looked at each of them, but they said nothing, so he took a sip of tea and continued.

"Eventually, my wife got tired of living this way and divorced me. I came home even less after that. What I'm trying to say is that I saw my daughter–her name is Laryssa–I saw her very little as she was growing up. She became a teenager and I hardly knew her. Once when she was about thirteen or fourteen I did come home over Christmas to see her, but it was as if I was a stranger, which I guess I was. We talked for a while, with lots of awkward silences, and whenever I tried to talk about her life she just closed up. It really was no business of mine, in her eyes, and I guess she was right.

"Anyway, about two years ago I got a text from my ex-wife that our daughter had disappeared. The police investigated, but she hasn't been found. We don't know what happened to her. We don't think she ran away because she had a good relationship with her mother, and she disappeared from the social media she was almost obsessed with. Eventually the police put her disappearance into a file with the thousands of other kids that just vanish."

Patty reached over and put her hand on Michael's arm in a gesture of quiet empathy. Michael acknowledged the kindness with a nod of the eyes and a slight smile.

"I left the military and got involved with CSR because I hoped that somehow at some point I'd hear something that would give me a clue as to where she might be. I've never given up hope that she's alive and that I'll find her. I think everyday that if I'd been a better father, if I'd been more involved in her life, if I'd been there when she was growing up, this wouldn't have happened."

Caleb and Patty listened intently despite their weariness. They felt deeply sorry for Michael who was fighting back tears and obviously anguished by his loss.

"Where was Laryssa living when she disappeared," Patty asked.

Michael didn't answer right away. He looked at Patty and then at Caleb. "Here. In Baltimore. About ten blocks from here."

The couple was startled by the proximity of Laryssa's presumed abduction, but they said nothing.

"When I learned of Alicia's disappearance, and that it was so close to where Laryssa disappeared from, I thought there might be a connection. It was a thin straw, I know, but it was something."

There was silence in the living room for maybe fifteen seconds. Michael stared at the floor biting his lip and holding back tears while the Hoffmeyers watched him, wishing there was something they could say or do to ease his heartache, but they knew from their own experience that there wasn't.

At length Patty broke the silence, "Michael, would you mind if we prayed for you and Laryssa?"

Michael was a bit taken aback. These people were going through their own personal agony, he thought, but they were able even so to be genuinely concerned about him. It was very kind. He agreed to Patty's suggestion, though he hadn't prayed since he was a boy in Sunday school. The three bereaved parents bowed their heads while Caleb prayed for Laryssa, Alicia, and Michael.

"Thank you," Michael said softly when Caleb had finished, "I appreciate your kindness and your prayers."

Caleb spent the next ten minutes recounting to Michael everything he knew about Alicia's disappearance, which wasn't much, and everything the police had been able to tell him, which also wasn't much. He told him that he regretted that he didn't have more information to provide, but he hoped something in what he said might eventually prove useful.

Michael thanked them both and promised to be in touch as soon as he heard anything about their daughter. Caleb assured him while walking him to the door that he and Patty would continue to pray for Laryssa.

Just before he left he turned to the couple. "There's one thing else maybe you can do, if you don't mind. The team in Mexico learned from their source that somebody by the name of Enrico Gardonez may have been involved in Alicia's kidnapping. I'm going to see that the police get that name, but if it should ever turn up would you let me know? Maybe this Enrico person knows something about Laryssa as well."

They assured him they would do as he asked as they accompanied him out onto their front porch.

"He's carrying a lot grief," Patty observed as they watched Michael make his way to his car. "Yeah," Caleb agreed, "and a lot of guilt, too."

Suddenly Michael stopped on the sidewalk and looked at his phone. He turned and strode quickly back up the steps to where the Hoffmeyers were still standing on the porch. Caleb met him with a puzzled look.

Michael smiled and held up the phone. "I just got a text from the guys in Mexico. They've rescued Alicia."

Long before the first rays of sunlight were visible over the hills east of Cumpas the town's roosters and dogs broke into a cacophony of crowing and barking. Smells of breakfast from a hundred outdoor stoves wafted through the cool morning air. A light came on in the room in which the men had concluded Alicia was probably being held.

The three-man team deployed silently and inconspicuously around the cabin.

Soon the door opened and a man wearing a blazer over a T-shirt emerged from the room carrying a small dufflebag. He reached into his pocket for the keys and pressed the fob to unlock the car. As he turned to reenter the cabin, he felt the muzzle of a gun press firmly against the back of his neck. He froze in shock and fear.

"Silencio." The solitary word was whispered in a barely audible voice. A hand reached under his jacket and removed a handgun from a shoulder holster.

Two team members then appeared on either side of the open door. Weapons raised, they pivoted into the room. The companion of the man apprehended outside was taken completely by surprise as he emerged from the bathroom zipping up his pants.

Both of the men tasked with delivering Alicia to Felix Castro had been so thoroughly stunned by the sudden and unexpected appearance of armed men that they surrendered without resistance.

Alicia was sitting on the bed wearing the same clothes she had on the day she was taken from the street in Baltimore. Her blond hair was tousled and her clothes were dirty and disheveled, but she appeared to be unharmed. Her lower lip and chin quivered in fright as she clutched the bed sheet to her throat, not knowing who these new men were and what they had in store for her.

"Don't be afraid, Alicia." Carlos' voice was gentle and comforting. "We're Americans. We're going to take you back to your parents."

Despite his assurances the young girl was obviously frightened of the men with guns and began to sob.

"Did these men hurt you?" Colin asked the question while glaring at the two men who were about to be trussed up in a fashion similar to that of the men left at the *hacienda* the previous day. The thugs had little doubt that their fate depended upon her answer.

"No," she answered in a quavering voice between sobs and sniffles, "they didn't hurt me."

Carlos took her by the hand and led her to the car while his teammates instructed her two captors to strip naked. Their mouths were taped, and they were left in the dingy room fastened securely to the pipes. Their clothes were stuffed into a pillowcase and thrown in the back of the car. Their weapons, keys, and phones were seized along with whatever cash they were carrying. Gas was siphoned out of their car into the five gallon plastic containers which had been partially emptied to fuel the drive the previous night.

It'd be a while before Castro's goons would be able to alert any of their friends who might be in the area. By then the team should be safely on their way to the American consulate in Hermosillo. As they drove out of Cumpas, Carlos breathed a silent sigh of relief that no triggers were pulled and that the rescue had gone as smoothly as it had. He wasn't sure that the other guys in the car felt the same way. He took out his phone to text John in Baltimore and the team at Cuidad Juarez that they had secured Alicia. He considered allowing

Alicia to call her parents but decided to just wait until she was safely turned over to the consulate.

Not far out of Cumpas they found themselves stopped at a railroad crossing as a freight train rumbled past. The delay made them nervous, but their attention was captured by what appeared in the grey, crepuscular light to be shapes on the tops of the box cars. They soon realized that the shapes were people, dozens of them, maybe more, heading north toward the border to try to sneak into the United States in search of a better life.

The CSR team watched silently until the train passed, and they were able to continue their drive toward Hermosillo. None of them liked that people were sneaking into the States. All of them thought the border was too easy to cross, that the flow of illegal immigration had to be curtailed, and they couldn't understand why their government wasn't doing more to stop it. It was almost funny, Carlos, thought to himself, that some of those who wanted the borders to the country to be left open to anyone who wanted to come in nevertheless lock their own homes and cars to prevent unwanted guests. His own grandparents had immigrated legally and he thought everyone else should, too, but he knew that were he in the same economic circumstances as so many of those people riding that train he'd probably be doing the same thing they were.

An hour or so further along, Carlos had Tyrone pull over at a roadside market. He jumped out and returned after about ten minutes with breakfast for everybody and a stuffed teddy bear, which, to Alicia's great delight, was a gift for her. Until that moment the young girl had been tense and fearful. She was alone in a car with three strange men and didn't really know whether she could trust them, but the gift of the teddy bear caused much of her suspicion and nervousness to melt away.

The team followed the same procedure Erin utilized in Cuidad Juarez except they decided to employ nuns as the go-between with the consulate. They located a convent in the city, and Carlos took Alicia, clutching her stuffed animal, to see the Mother Superior while the others remained in the car. He explained who Alicia was, what she'd been through, and why he needed to ask Mother to take the girl to the American consulate and explain all this herself to the consulate personnel. The Mother Superior eyed Carlos suspiciously.

"Did this man hurt you?" she asked Alicia while protectively drawing the girl close to her.

"No," Alicia replied, holding tightly to her teddy bear. "He saved me."

Still wary of the man with the pony-tail and his strangely vague description of the circumstances that brought him and the girl to her door, she nevertheless agreed to help, and a car and driver were summoned.

Carlos also gave the nun a piece of paper to give to the Consul General explaining what they knew about Felix Castro and his human trafficking operation.

The Mother Superior entered the consulate with Alicia and explained to the receptionist who Alicia was. The receptionist immediately called the Consul General who in turn contacted the FBI. Within hours Alicia had called her parents, showered, been fed, examined by a doctor, and interviewed by an FBI agent who was curious not only about the details of her kidnapping, but also the details of her rescue and who the mysterious men were who carried it out.

There wasn't much Alicia could tell the agent, a tall woman in her thirties who looked like she might have played basketball in college, about the people who rescued her except that they were Americans, they had guns, and they caught her kidnappers by surprise. She also assured the agent that the kidnappers didn't hurt her nor were they hurt by her rescuers. She recounted to the agent that she rode in the car for several hours with the men who brought her here from a town whose name she didn't know to the convent in Hermosillo, but other than asking her from time to time if she was hungry or had to go to the bathroom, the only thing her rescuers asked her for was information about how she was abducted in Baltimore.

Alicia told the agent what she told her rescuers. "I was walking down the street a couple blocks from my house on the way to a party for a girl in my class at school. A car came up behind me and a man jumped out and grabbed me and dragged me into the back seat. They took my purse and phone, tied something over my eyes, and the next thing I knew I was waking up in a strange house where the men all spoke Spanish. I knew there were other children in the house, but I was tied to a bed and never had a chance to talk to them.

"I was there for a day and a night. They brought me food twice and took me to the bathroom three or four times. I cried most of the time. The next day two other men came and took me. When we went outside they didn't blindfold me so I could see that where we were wasn't any place like Baltimore. We drove for a long time and stopped at a place to eat and sleep. The men talked to each other but not to me, and my Spanish isn't good enough to know what they were saying. Then those other men came this morning with guns and rescued me and brought me here."

The next morning Alicia was taken to Hermosillo Airport and, accompanied by the FBI agent, flown to Baltimore-Washington Airport via Atlanta.

When Michael announced the news to Caleb and Patty that Alicia had been rescued they were shocked, grateful, and delirious with joy all at once. Overcome with emotion they hugged each other, hugged Michael, thanked him profusely, cried copiously, and poured out a prayer of thanks right there on their front porch. Then they sank onto the steps, buried their faces in each other's shoulders and cried.

Michael touched Patty lightly on the shoulder and quietly withdrew.

Their grief had been like a heavy, oppressive darkness, a palpable gloom that seemed almost personal, as if evil itself had taken the form of a conscious being surrounding them and crushing their hearts and their spirits. In an instant they felt it all evaporate. Their joy and elation couldn't be put into words. It was offset only by their awareness that for so many parents in similar situations, parents like Michael, there is no happy ending.

Several hours later they received a call from the FBI confirming what Michael had told them, assuring them that their daughter was safely in the hands of consulate personnel in Hermosillo, and that she was apparently unharmed.

As soon as they heard from the FBI they got on their phones and started calling everyone who'd been supporting them to share the news. The response from almost everyone was the same: "It's a miracle!"

It wasn't long after that Alicia called them on FaceTime from the consulate and all the emotion that had accompanied the initial word of her rescue flooded over them again as though a levee in their hearts had burst. They showered her image on the phone with kisses and tears, struggling to find words to express the joy and love they were feeling.

Now they had come to Thurgood Marshall/BWI airport, south of the city, accompanied by numerous friends from the neighborhood, work, and church, all of whom impatiently awaited the arrival of Alicia's flight. Caleb and Patty were still so overwhelmed they had to lean on each other for support. Their only child, their little girl, was coming home. They had feared the worst, they'd been through almost every emotion a parent could experience during the last week, and when they saw Alicia running toward them the tears flowed and the hugs and kisses lasted for ten full minutes.

Their gratitude for this wonderful gift was boundless. They heaped profuse thanks upon the FBI agent who had escorted her. The agent accepted it politely, but thought to herself that there are some mysterious, anonymous men somewhere in Mexico who are the ones who deserve the thanks.

Forty-five minutes later Loren and Olivia Holt drove out of the day-use parking lot close to the terminal and headed west on I-195 toward home. They were almost giddy with happiness for the Hoffmeyers.

Everyone agreed to allow the family to spend that evening together with each other, but they'd also decided while waiting at the airport that they'd have a reception at the church on Friday night for everyone who had supported them during their ordeal.

Loren was thinking about the preparations for that event and also mulling over something that Caleb had passed on to him while they were awaiting Alicia's flight. Caleb had mentioned that during the visit in which Michael had received the news about Alicia's rescue he related to Caleb that he'd been given the name of Enrico Gardonez as a possible suspect in Alicia's abduction. The pastor, who knew a lot of people in the neighborhoods surrounding his church, was trying to recall whether he'd ever heard that name before, but he couldn't come up with anything.

As he turned their brand new Toyota Yaris onto northbound I-295 enroute to Baltimore, Olivia asked him what he thought, theologically speaking, about the men who engaged in the trade of buying and selling girls for the sex trade.

"I guess what I'm wondering is, what's hell going to be like for those terrible men?" There was no doubt in her mind that hell was where such men were headed, she just wondered what the experience would consist of. "In fact, I guess I'm wondering what hell's like, period," she clarified.

Loren smiled and exhaled a short *hmm*. "That's a good question, hon. I'm sure no one really knows. At least no one who's *alive* knows." His reply came with an arched brow and a wry smile.

"Well, you're the pastor, Loren. What do you *think*?"

The question sloshed around in her husband's mind for a moment or two. "Well, I think hell's what comes of rejecting God's love and forgiveness, so in some sense a person in hell is someone who has chosen it for himself. He chooses to be isolated from God."

"But how can that be if God is everywhere?" Olivia interrupted.

Loren checked the left lane, making sure it was clear to pull out to pass the pokey car in front of him. "Maybe it's like this: Being in hell is like being confined to a tiny point, a kind of infinitesimally small prison that floats around in the mind of God but is somehow quarantined, like a virus in a computer. Or kind of like dust motes floating in the air. They're all around us, but we're oblivious to them, and they're completely inconsequential to us.

"Maybe hell is like being forever in this kind of solitary confinement but surrounded by the presence of God and unable to escape it. For someone who detests God and detests the idea of spending eternity with him, that would certainly be a torment, don't you think?"

Olivia stared out into the night as she pondered Loren's theory.

"So you're saying that maybe heaven and hell are the same place, but people in hell are trapped in the dust motes?" The idea amused her, and she endeavored unsuccessfully to suppress a giggle as she asked the question.

Loren glanced over at her and laughed himself. "You think that idea's silly, don't you?" It was more of a statement than a question.

"No," Olivia fibbed, grinning, "I just never heard it put that way before."

He knew his conjecture sounded a little far-fetched, but it was the best he could do. He believed hell was real. He believed that unless it was real there could be no justice, nor any moral law. You can have neither law nor justice unless people are somehow held accountable for what they do and for the choices they make, but what hell was, exactly, and whether a person was "there" forever, he could do no better than speculate.

"One thing I'm pretty sure of, though, hon. Beauty and goodness are absent from hell, there's only eternal bleakness. Beauty and good emanate from the nature of God. He's their source. They have no existence apart from him."

Loren reflected on this a little more as he drove. He darted a sideways peek at his wife and grinned as though pleased to have the opportunity to expatiate on a theological theme that didn't arise very often among his clerical colleagues nor in his everyday duties as a pastor.

"So you think," Olivia asked, "that whoever winds up there does so because they choose it? He doesn't put anyone there? They're there because they don't want to be with him? But how does someone make a choice like that? Why *would* they?" The thought ran through Olivia's mind that if God is the source of all that's good, the source of beauty, love, and truth, who wouldn't prefer that to its opposite?

"Maybe a person's life stands as his or her choice," Loren said in response to her questions. "Maybe when we die God asks us just one question. He asks simply, 'Do you love me?' And our whole life stands as our answer. Maybe there are some people so sick

and perverse that they'll be nauseated standing in the presence of absolute Goodness and want to get away from it. But it's their choice. God doesn't force himself on anyone."

Olivia had a hard time understanding why someone would deliberately choose hell over heaven. "Wouldn't everyone want to be in heaven if they knew that heaven existed?"

"I don't know, hon. Eyes accustomed to darkness are pained by light. They're repelled by it toward the darkness. They prefer it. Besides, why do people reject God in *this* life?" For Loren it seemed evident that if people don't want to be with God in this life they probably wouldn't want to be with him in the next, either.

"Maybe they don't reject him so much as they just don't believe he's there," his wife ventured.

"Maybe, but I think most people believe he's there, but they don't want him to be, so they refuse to acknowledge him. I read a quote from a philosopher who said that he doesn't believe because he just doesn't want God to exist. Another guy, a top scientist, wrote that the reason he believes in evolution is because he doesn't want to believe that there's a creator.

"There probably are a lot of reasons why people don't believe in God, but I think that simply not wanting there to be a God is near the top of the list. Atheism may be more psychological than rational."

Olivia pondered that for a moment. "And those men who took Alicia? What about them?" she asked.

"I don't know, Olivia, but maybe it's like this: When we're young God stands right in front of us, tells us he loves us and holds out his hand. Maybe we take it, maybe we don't, but if we don't we back away from him a step or two. At some point God asks us again to come back and take his hand. Maybe we do, maybe we don't, but if we don't we move even further away. If we keep saying 'no' to him we wind up so far away that we no longer even hear his voice telling us he loves us and urging us to come back. We just keep drifting further and further away until it's almost impossible to get back to him even if we wanted to."

Olivia was finding this fascinating. She thought it odd that in all the dinner table conversations she'd had with her husband over the years on matters of philosophy, theology and everything else, somehow this topic had never come up.

"Why did you say a moment ago that for there to be justice there has to be a hell?" The questions were crowding into Olivia's mind, and she wanted to ask them before they arrived home and were busied with other matters.

"Well, I guess that if the fate of someone who tortures and murders little children turns out to be the same as that of the children he's tortured and murdered then reality is fundamentally unjust. If there are no real consequences for evil then I'm not even sure evil would be evil.

"I guess I don't see how justice can be anything but an illusion if death is the end of our existence and if men who have caused so much pain and suffering are never held accountable for what they did. If atheists are right then the world is an absurdity and so is any attempt to live a moral life. It's all utterly meaningless. Unless what we do matters forever, it doesn't matter at all.

"It's funny in a way," Loren appended as an afterthought, "that modern skeptics talk a lot about justice as though it were a moral imperative without realizing that if they're right about God not existing and there being no life after death then there are no moral imperatives. No real justice either."

Olivia was moving on to another question that she wanted to insert into her mix of wonderings. "One other thing I've always been puzzled about. If hell exists, is it forever? Are people there forever?"

Loren took a deep breath, adjusted the heater, and shifted his position in his seat before he answered. Olivia suspected that he might be reluctant to deal with her question.

"Here's what I think about that, hon. Hell for a person only lasts as long as justice demands. If the purpose of any punishment is to cure our inclination to evil then an eternal punishment without any hope of relief or remediation would be counterproductive and unjust. It would only make the people suffering it hate and resent God more.

I think he wants everyone's love, even the love of those in hell. If that's so, then maybe it's not forever, maybe it's only so long as the person remains defiant. Maybe there's a point when at least some people finally recognize their rebellion for what it is and submit to God and accept his love and forgiveness. Maybe. Anyway, I *hope* so, I think *everybody* should hope so, but I just don't know."

It sometimes occurred to Loren that we're like young children who at their stage of maturity lack the conceptual apparatus to comprehend mathematics. In our limited humanity we lack the conceptual apparatus to comprehend God. Perhaps the ability develops somewhat as we mature and think about him more, but time runs out in life before we get very far. Like a parent who answers a child's questions by saying "you wouldn't understand," maybe God has to tell us when we try to delve too deeply into the way things ultimately are that we just wouldn't understand, and we have to be satisfied with that.

Soon they were pulling into their garage. Any more talk of such things would have to wait until they were lying together in bed later that night. For now their thoughts turned once again to plans for the reception that would be held at the church in a couple of days.

The three members of the team who stayed behind at the safehouse closed the place up, packed Luis—whom they had blindfolded and immobilized with plastic handcuffs and ankle shackles—into the car and eventually deposited him on the doorstep of the federal police in Cuidad Juarez. A note was fastened around his neck enumerating his various crimes, particularly his role in the trafficking of children. Tape of his interrogation was placed in an envelope and deposited in the drop box. A copy was mailed to the American consulate. Unless he managed to bribe someone he would probably spend at least a few years in prison.

Then, as did the three men who had rescued Alicia, the team disbanded and exfiltrated out of Mexico back to the states.

Most of the team members returned to their jobs and families, but Danny and Carlos had no such obligations. Michael invited them to come to Baltimore to help him track down the mysterious Enrico Gardonez, and the two CSR agents, having nothing more important to do, accepted.

Michael planned to anonymously slip Gardonez's name to the FBI, but as long as there was a chance the man might know something about his daughter's disappearance, he wanted to remain in Baltimore just in case there was something he could do to help find him.

CHAPTER SIX

The church social hall, festooned with bunting, balloons, and home-made banners, was filled with people welcoming Alicia home. Some sentiment had been expressed that all the fuss might be overwhelming for the young girl who was shy like her mother, but her parents allayed those concerns and assured their friends that she'd be just fine as long as the media didn't try to make her into a celebrity. Given what she'd been through she was remarkably unscathed, as far as anyone could tell.

There were a couple hundred well-wishers milling about the hall taking advantage of the punch and pastries buffet and conveying their love and joy to each member of the Hoffmeyer family.

About a half hour into the evening Caleb's phone sounded, and Michael's name appeared on the screen. Patty had called Michael and John the previous day to invite them to the reception. John couldn't make it, but Michael accepted and intimated that he might have a surprise for them. Now he was on the phone telling Caleb that he wanted to see the family but was concerned that there'd be a lot of media at the reception, which there were, and maybe even some police hanging around, and he hoped there might be a room where he could visit quietly and unobtrusively with them for just a few minutes.

Caleb directed him to an inconspicuous entrance where he could meet him and escort him to the church parlor, a room suitably furnished for small gatherings. Michael asked that Patty and Alicia wait for them in the parlor while Caleb let him into the building and that Caleb not tell his family what was going on. He wanted his visit to be a surprise.

Caleb excused himself from the party, promising to bring Alicia right back, and motioned to Loren to come with him. He whispered to Holt that something strange was afoot, but aside from the fact that it involved Michael, he had no idea what it was. He sent Patty and Alicia upstairs to the parlor while he and Loren went to open a side door of the old church building.

As Caleb approached the door he could peer through the glass into the darkness outside and discern that Michael was accompanied by two other men. It didn't occur to him that they were the surprise. When the men entered the church, Michael was smiling but he held up his hand as if to forestall introductions. He said only that he'd explain when he saw Alicia.

Patty and Alicia couldn't understand why they had to sit in the parlor or what all the mystery was about, but when the parlor door opened and three men walked in ahead of Caleb and Loren, Alicia's eyes grew wide. Rising excitedly out of her chair she ran to the men. One of them was Michael, one was a complete stranger to everyone, and the third, the man with the pony-tail, broke into a wide grin as he saw Alicia, still clinging tightly to the stuffed bear she'd scarcely relinquished since she'd arrived home, running across the room toward him. Carlos raised her in his arms and they hugged, much to the astonishment of her mother who only slowly began to realize who this stranger was.

The third man with Michael and Carlos was Danny Howe.

When Caleb and Patty learned that these were the men who had rescued their daughter they were overcome once more with emotion and gratitude. They couldn't thank them enough for what they had done for their daughter.

At length Caleb introduced Michael to Loren Holt who remembered Michael from his visit to the Hoffmeyer's home about a week before. Michael in turn introduced Carlos and Danny, explaining, though by this time no explanation was necessary, that they were part of the team that had rescued Alicia. They'd come to Baltimore at his invitation, and while they were there they wanted to see Alicia.

"You're a preacher?" Carlos inquired of Loren when the initial commotion had subsided and someone mentioned that he was Alicia's pastor. "Maybe we should talk." As he spoke these words Carlos turned and looked at Danny.

His proposal took Loren by surprise. "Sure. I'd be glad to talk with you," he said. "I don't know how you guys did what you did, but you've certainly made a lot of people very happy."

Carlos smiled enigmatically. "We had a lot of good luck."

"And a lot of prayers," Caleb added.

"I'm sure we did," Carlos agreed. "Perhaps that's why we had a lot of luck. But that's not what we'd like to talk with you about."

"Well, if there's something I can help you with I'll be in my office down the hall until about two tomorrow afternoon and every morning next week. Feel free to stop by."

After a few more minutes the three men began to leave. Caleb had a hundred questions he wanted to ask these men about the rescue, but there wasn't time on this night.

Alicia gave Carlos one last hug. He pointed to Danny and said she should hug him, too, that Danny was the one who wheedled the information out of their "informant" that led to them finding her. Alicia complied with hugs for everyone. Michael smiled, but there was sadness in his eyes. He envied the Hoffmeyers' joy and longed for the same kind of reunion with his own daughter.

Loren had enormous admiration for these men who had risked their lives to save a little girl they didn't even know from a life of unspeakable evil. They truly were heroes. He felt small in their presence, and he wondered why in the world they would want to talk to him.

An hour later the crowd was thinning in the social hall. Loren relaxed in a folding chair at one of the tables, sipping from a cup of punch and nibbling on a cookie.

Willis Hoffmeyer walked over and seated himself in a chair across from him. His wife Marie joined them a few moments later. Loren's wife Olivia was helping in the kitchen.

Loren leaned back in his chair and looked across the table at Willis. "I regret that it took the terrible events of the last week or so to get you into a church, Willis," he chided the literature prof with an impish grin.

"It may be the last time I'm in one for a while," Willis riposted with a grin of his own. Loren was attracted to Willis' amiability. He seemed genuinely warm, unlike Marie whose smiles struck Loren as cold, mirthless and perfunctory. "Please don't think I'm trying to be disrespectful, Pastor, but the answers to life's questions aren't likely to be found in a church building."

It was unusual in Loren's experience to encounter someone as forthright, even eager, to challenge him on the intellectual legitimacy of both his faith and his profession as Willis seemed to be. He knew there were many people like Willis, of course, or at least he supposed there were, but he just never encountered very many. Most people who shared Willis' attitude toward Christianity simply didn't care to talk about it, at least not with him, but Loren thought the 18th century British man of letters Samuel Johnson was on the mark when he wrote that it's astonishing, given the importance of the question, that anyone should think of anything else.

It wasn't too much of an exaggeration, he mused, to judge almost everything else people do, think about, or talk about, as not much more than a distraction, an attempt to paper over our existential emptiness. If one concludes that there is no God then, it seemed to Loren, everything else in life must be viewed through the lens of one's inevitable death and annihilation, which was pretty depressing.

Willis was an interesting antagonist. He gave Loren the impression that it was important to him to convince Loren that he, Willis, was right and that Loren was mistaken. In this respect Willis was much the mirror image of Loren himself who believed it important to explain to doubters why it was eminently rational to believe in God's existence and the truth of the gospel, and that this belief was more intellectually profound and satisfying than was the *de facto* atheism largely embraced by much of modern society.

Unlike Willis, however, Loren rarely introduced theological or philosophical topics into conversation with those he thought likely to disagree with him. To do so made people uncomfortable and defensive which, he'd learned over the years, did not make for an atmosphere conducive to fruitful dialogue. He was content to let the questions which most interested him be raised by others so that they felt themselves to be partners in a discussion rather than the quarry of a Christian bounty hunter. Holt didn't try to convert people, and didn't see that as something he could achieve in any case. He just didn't want to let objections to Christianity go unchallenged lest the objector infer from his silence that there were no answers to the objections.

Loren looked across the table at Willis and willingly rose to the bait the professor had dangled in front of him.

"Where *are* the answers found, Willis?"

Willis smiled. "To the extent they can be found at all, Loren, they're discovered by our reason."

Loren cast his eyes down at the cookie on the white paper table covering. He scooped some crumbs off the table with the edge of his hand and, without looking up, muttered that while religion without reason leads to fanaticism, reason without religion leads to despair. He then looked at Willis with a crinkled smile, "I don't know if somebody said that or if I just made it up."

Willis was not deterred by what seemed to him, mistakenly, to be Holt's disinclination to take his words seriously.

"Religion is based on faith and faith requires us to ignore the evidence or to believe when there is no evidence, Pastor, and I just think that's a sin against the mind. It's wrong to believe anything on insufficient evidence," Willis continued, "and that's what Christians do. There's no evidence that there's a God so the Christian just decides that he'll take it on faith that there is. Not only is *that* wrong, it's also immoral to continue to believe without considering the arguments against one's belief."

Loren was leaning back in his chair with his legs crossed, a cup of punch in one hand. He took a sip and placed the cup on the table.

"I don't think that's what faith is at all, Willis. What you've defined, belief without evidence, is *blind* faith, but Christian faith isn't blind. It's not belief despite the lack of evidence, it's belief, or better, a *trust*, despite the lack of *proof*, which is a different matter altogether. There's actually plenty of *evidence* for the basic claims of Christian theism."

Loren continued his thought before Willis could respond.

"But in any case, you say that it's immoral to believe anything on insufficient evidence. Do you mind if I ask you a couple of questions about that, Willis?"

"Go ahead." Willis was curious to hear what questions Holt would pose to him. He didn't imagine they'd be difficult to answer.

"Okay. First, you obviously believe what you just told me, that it's wrong to believe without sufficient evidence, but what evidence do you have that *that* claim is itself true? If you *believe* it's true you must have some evidence to support it, Willis, but I don't think you do. In fact I don't think you *can*. I suspect that you take it on faith, *blind* faith, in fact, that it's true."

Willis started to reply but thought better of it because he really didn't have a good answer. He wanted to say that everyone has to accept certain axioms by faith or else reason would have nothing to work on, but he knew that if he admitted that it was rational to believe something to be true even though it couldn't be demonstrated, Loren would ask him why a believer wasn't rational to consider the existence of God an axiom one could accept even though it couldn't be demonstrated to everyone's satisfaction. Rather than give Loren that opening he let the question pass and waited for a more promising opportunity.

Willis shifted in his seat and focused his eyes intently on Loren. "What's your second question?" He chuckled, as if tacitly conceding Loren's first point.

"My second question is, what would you consider to be sufficient evidence that God exists? It seems to me that there's enough evidence, to quote Pascal, to convince anyone who's not dead set against it, but apparently there's not enough to convince *you*, so I'm wondering what it would take for you to change your mind."

Loren's question was rhetorical. He was pretty sure he knew the answer. Unbelief, he suspected, was only infrequently the result of a due consideration of evidence. He sometimes reflected to himself that the heavens could open and God appear to the whole world thundering, "Now you have no justification left for your unbelief," and people would still say, "Oh, yeah? What about all those starving children in Africa?"

Willis' response was pretty much exactly that. He felt this question was a slow, hanging curve ball that he could knock out of the park.

"For starters," he replied, "there'd have to be a lot less pain in the world. You believe that God is all-powerful and perfectly good, but what good parent would stand by and let his children suffer if he had the power to stop it or prevent it, Loren? The fact that God lets little kids be bought and sold by those thugs who kidnapped Alicia is appalling if he could stop it and yet doesn't."

Loren expected this argument would make an appearance sooner or later in this discussion. In his mind the problem of suffering is the most formidable argument against theism since it's difficult to reconcile the pointless suffering of a child, or even an animal, with the existence of a loving, all-powerful Father. Although Loren believed the argument's strength lies more in its emotional effect than in its logical rigor, it was not an argument he dismissed lightly.

"I don't pretend to have a convincing answer to that question, Willis. It's a vexing problem, but it's also kind of peculiar in a way."

"Why is that?" Willis was pleased that he seemed to have discomfited the pastor.

"What I mean is that one of the arguments people sometimes make against miracles is that God couldn't intervene in the natural order to perform miracles because that would create havoc with the laws of physics. There'd be no way to predict that one event will cause another if God sometimes overrode the laws of nature. In other words, if miracles happen they'd make science a very difficult enterprise, if not altogether impossible."

Loren paused and Willis looked at him with an expression that implied that he didn't see how this had anything to do with his question. Loren smiled slightly and glanced down at the table.

"At least, that's what people say, but then those folks turn around and criticize God, or at least the concept of God, because he doesn't intervene continuously and constantly to prevent men from doing evil. Every one of the interventions they say God should perform to prevent evil would be a miracle. So the skeptic criticizes the idea of a miracle-working God because that would produce chaos, and then he criticizes the idea of a benevolent, omnipotent God because he *doesn't* work miracles. I think that's trying to have it both ways."

Willis began to say something, but Loren held up a finger and asked to add one more thought.

"I think we have to remember that the fact that there are a couple of tough problems in Christian theology isn't in itself a good reason to conclude that Christian theism is false any more than the fact that there seem to be irreconcilable contradictions in physics between quantum mechanics and relativity theory is a good reason for scientists to abandon physics."

"Well, look," Willis replied calmly, once again shifting his weight in his chair, "the question of what evidence it would take to make me believe isn't really the important issue, in any case. The fact is that God's just not necessary to explain the world. We know that man wasn't invented, that he evolved. We know that we're not at the center of the universe. We can explain everything in terms of matter and energy. There's no room left in the modern belief system for God. He's unnecessary. You think you need to believe in God in order to know the answers. I think that's just wrong." His voice was soft but firm.

Willis looked at Loren with an expression that implied that the matter was pretty much settled for him, he had made his choice years ago, and changing course now would be like trying to change the course of an aircraft carrier with an oar. Loren suspected that nothing he could say would alter that. He wished, however, to clarify what he thought was a misunderstanding on Willis' part.

"It's not that if there is a God in whom one believes that the believer will then know the answers, Willis. It's that if there is no God then there just are no answers. At least no answers to those really important questions you referred to a minute ago."

Willis was dubious. His expression conveyed genuine puzzlement. "How can you say that, Loren? What real-world questions can you as a Christian answer that an atheist can't?"

Loren leaned forward and rested his arms on the table. This was for him one of the most important matters anyone could think about: What does the world look like if atheism is true? He felt that too few people really take the time to think about the logical endpoint of their basic assumptions about God. If there is no God then what follows? Loren believed that that question is crucial because few people who want to reject belief in God are really willing to live with the logical consequences of that rejection. They piggyback on the Christian worldview while denying that they're doing any such thing.

His eyes passed from Willis to Marie, whose face had adopted a sullen expression since she had joined them at the table, and back to her husband. Loren then offered his opinion.

"Well, one question that I think a theist can answer that an atheist can't is the question why we should care about others. On atheism, why would it be wrong to live selfishly? Why would it be wrong to ignore the poverty or suffering of people you could otherwise help? Why would it be wrong to squander the world's resources on ourselves and let future generations fend for themselves?

"Another question is whether there's any real purpose to all our striving to manage disappointment, regret, guilt, pain, and existential emptiness. Life's a continual search for something, anything, that would make our lives even a little bit meaningful. If God doesn't exist and death is the end of our existence then none of it means anything. It's all just a pointless flicker. Like Camus said, 'For the man who is alone without God, the weight of days is dreadful.'"

Neither Willis nor Marie were moved by Loren's words.

"Look, we don't need God for life to be meaningful, Loren," Marie answered somewhat patronizingly. "We can find meaning in work and relationships." She said it as though explaining a simple truth to a child. Willis nodded slightly in agreement.

Loren didn't respond. He tapped his empty paper cup lightly on the table and thought about a literature professor he once had who devoted most of his adult life to publishing papers and books in which he argued that Shakespeare didn't really write Hamlet. If that's the way Willis' career was spent he wondered in what sense that sort of work could really be meaningful, but he was too polite to voice the thought.

"Why do you think God is necessary for meaning, Loren?" Marie pressed.

Loren hesitated for a second as he watched the last of his parishioners shaking hands with Caleb and Patty. After a moment's pause he returned his attention to Marie whose question brought to his mind the words of the novelist Evelyn Waugh who wrote that life is both unintelligible and unendurable without God.

"Listen. I don't wish to be a melancholy voice on this joyous occasion, but, you know, some people find meaning in collecting stamps, others in photographing butterflies, others in going on shopping trips, but I don't see how any of those things at the moment of death, when we face utter extinction, are objectively meaningful. At that point nothing we've done in life matters. At least not if, at that point, we really do stand on the brink of total annihilation.

"The man who believes his death is the end but who still thinks the pleasures of life are somehow meaningful is like a condemned man who insists on weeding his garden before being hauled off to the gallows, or like a baseball team that's been eliminated from contention by mid-season playing out a string of 'meaningless games.' That's sort of the situation I think we're in if when we die it's the end of our existence. We're just playing out the string. We're like old men playing checkers in the park to pass the time until we die. There's no real meaning, or purpose, or significance to it. At least, I don't see how there can be."

"Goodness," exclaimed Marie, her irises disappearing into the tops of her eye sockets, "such a pessimistic view of life. I can't imagine that if your sermons reflect those views that you have many people in the pews on Sunday morning." Her tone was teasing, but it also had a barb buried in it.

Holt smiled. He had to agree that he did sound a little morose, but he was also persuaded that in a Godless universe life is little more than an attempt to find something to do to occupy ourselves until we shuffle off this mortal coil. He was convinced, though, that in fact we're not extinguished at death, and therefore everything we do really does matter because it lasts for eternity.

Caleb, Patty, and Alicia said good-bye to the last of their well-wishers and ambled over to the table where their pastor was engaged with Willis and Marie in what was evidently a serious conversation. All three sat down as Willis joined his wife in insisting that Loren was mistaken about his assessment of the meaninglessness of human existence.

"Well, I just don't think that's right, Loren. I take a great deal of pleasure from my writing and my teaching. They give me all the meaning and purpose I need to have a satisfying life. God isn't necessary."

"Maybe so, Willis, I certainly wouldn't claim that your teaching isn't satisfying, but I once knew a man, a writer whose name you'd probably recognize, who told me that he came to a point in his life where he suddenly realized that his work, his art, his writing was all just a frantic attempt to grasp some significance while he could, and he was haunted by the fear that a decade after his death it wouldn't mean anything at all to anyone. He said to me, 'If a life that only lasts six minutes is meaningless, why is a life that lasts sixty years any less so?' It was an intriguing question.

"In fact, lots of writers and other thoughtful people have come to the same conclusion, as I'm sure you're aware. Sartre put it pretty concisely, I think, when he said that, 'Life ceases to have meaning the moment we lose the illusion of being eternal.' Dostoyevsky said much the same thing. In *The Possessed* he has Kirillov say, 'I can't understand how an atheist can know there is no God and not kill himself on the spot.' "

Loren cocked his head, arched an eyebrow at Willis, and grinned wryly as he recited the passage, as if curious to see whether Willis was inclined to take Kirillov's words to heart.

Willis, for his part, was mildly charmed by Holt's fondness for literary references. In his experience it was unusual to find a clergyman who was intelligent, educated, and culturally sophisticated. Most clergy he'd known could quote the Bible and that was about it.

"You like Dostoyevsky?" he asked, changing the subject.

Loren nodded his assent. "I think he understood something important about the human condition. Why does he have Kirillov say that? Why does he have Ivan Karamazov say that without God everything is permitted and then go insane? Why does the atheist Raskolnikov murder the old women? I think Dostoyevsky sees that a Godless world is dark, depraved, nihilistic, and meaningless."

"But Dostoyevsky was a Christian, Loren. Of course he'd think that," Willis objected.

"Well, then, what about Camus? He wasn't a Christian. His cat-alog of atheistic nihilism in *The Rebel* is pretty chilling. What about Meursault, Camus' 'stranger,' whose life is utterly void of any real meaning and who kills a man for no reason?

"According to the modern narrative we're just atoms colliding in the void, Willis. How can there be any real meaning in what we do if that's all we are?

"Look," the pastor continued, leaning back in his chair once again, "if there's no afterlife then meaning is in the same predicament as jus-tice. There may be relatively minor restitutions for minor injustices, but, if there's no ultimate accountability, there's surely no justice for people who do great evils, who cause great suffering, nor is there jus-tice for their victims. Likewise, Willis, we may have minor projects and purposes which give us incentive to get out of bed in the morning, but unless these matter for eternity, all that we do is ultimately pur-poseless, and the meaning we assign to it is just an illusion."

Loren was not optimistic that an appeal to the meaninglessness of an empty universe would have much impact on Willis or Marie. That appeal seems to have purchase only on those who've experienced the emptiness themselves, who've felt it keenly deep in the marrow of their souls, and maybe that experience requires something of a melancholy temperament, the sort one tends to find in very sensitive people like writers and artists. The general run of mankind seems disposed to attribute whatever feelings of emptiness that might afflict them to some emotional or material lack in their lives, or, perhaps more often, to simply suppress the unpleasant intrusion altogether.

"I don't know about all that you're talking about," Patty inter-jected into the discussion. "All I know is that having our little girl back is an answer to prayer. This whole congregation was praying for her, and we got her back." She put her arm around Alicia and gave her the five thousandth hug she'd received that night. "That's proof enough for me."

Nobody said anything. It seemed somehow insensitive to gainsay her conviction, but Loren knew that Patty's reasoning would not sway people like her in-laws who'd surely view the attempt to connect Alicia's return to the prayers of the congregation as an instance of the *post hoc* fallacy. He thought it best to change the subject.

"Well," he said, turning to Alicia, "we're all thankful that you're back, honey."

"Me too," she replied with a cute little-girl grin. "I prayed a lot, too."

Patty smiled and excused herself and her daughter from the table to go help the folks in the kitchen finish cleaning up. Caleb remained seated beside his brother but added little to the conversation. He was content to merely take in the back and forth between Willis and Loren as they debated matters of belief and unbelief. He was also so happy tonight that entering into that debate just seemed somehow inappropriate, as though it would diminish his joy by diverting his attention from it.

The route Michael and his companions followed back to their hotel skirted the edge of one of the city's worst neighborhoods. At one point they drove within four blocks of an apartment in which a young woman sat on the edge of a bed holding another woman in her arms, gently rocking her back and forth as they both wept and prayed that God would somehow deliver them from their wretched circumstances. They were confined in a room from which there was no escape. Both had just been brutally assaulted by two men whose distant laughter rained down on them like cold sleet from a floor somewhere above them. The two women were living in hell and they cried desperately to God to be delivered from it.

CHAPTER SEVEN

Willis watched Patty and her daughter make their way toward the kitchen and then turned back to the table to continue his dialogue with Pastor Holt. He was invigorated by the challenge Holt presented, even if he wished he could counter Holt's arguments with more compelling rebuttals. He was accustomed to having his way when promoting his worldview among his students, but this preacher too often put him on the defensive, and though that was not a posture he found particularly comfortable, it was one he did find intellectually bracing. He was confident that whatever advantage Holt was enjoying was only temporary and that he would eventually turn the conversation in his favor. He enjoyed conversing with Holt even if he wasn't always aware that he did.

The professor took up a matter that had been bothering him since their exchange at his brother's home and to which Holt had just returned a few minutes before.

"You just said that there's no reason to care about others unless there's a God, Pastor. Do you mean to suggest that an atheist can't be a good person? Do you deny that Marie and I can be just as moral as anyone in your church even if we don't believe in God?"

"Of course you can, Willis," Loren responded, "but that's not the point. The point is that on atheism there's no moral obligation to be one way rather than another. You have no *duty* to care about others. You can live by whatever values you please, and had you chosen different values you wouldn't have been morally wrong to do so."

Both Willis and Marie looked skeptical so Loren tried an illustration.

"Look, when a non-believer says that he can live just as good a life as any Christian he's like a man who sits in a restaurant with his vegan friend looking over a menu filled with meat dishes. The special is a salad so the vegan says, 'I think I'll have the special.' The man says, 'Well, I can have the special, too, you know.' Of course he can, he can choose whatever he wants, but the point is that nothing he chooses would be 'wrong.' He has no obligation to select the salad. His choice is just a matter of personal preference."

"No, it's not," Willis objected, "at least informed morality's not based on personal preference. It's based on reason. Our reason guides us in moral matters and the rational man follows the dictates of his reason."

"Maybe so, Willis, but what does our reason dictate? It seems to me that reason tells us to put our own interests ahead of those of others, to look out for ourselves first. How do we decide through reason whether it's right to help poor people we don't know if it means sacrificing our own good to do so? How can reason decide between living for ourselves or living for others? How can reason tell Faustus it's wrong to sell his soul if doing so brings Faustus the power he craves?

"All reason does is show us the best way to achieve a goal, but it can't tell us whether the goal is morally right. The only way we can tell whether the goal is right is by comparing it to a higher standard, but unless there's a God there is no higher standard."

No response was forthcoming so Loren hastened to add another thought.

"We live in a world of human predators, Willis. People who have no guilt, no remorse, no regret–a world of Raskolnikovs and Meursaults and people like the ones who took Alicia. And why should they feel regret? The lion doesn't feel remorse or guilt when it kills the antelope. If everything we do is just the outworking of blind Darwinian processes and the laws of nature why should we regret what happens? If atheism is true then maybe the most morally consistent people in society are its sociopaths and psychopaths. They feel no guilt."

Marie managed to stifle a shudder of distaste for Holt's assertion. This Holt character, in her assessment, was a sophist, a charlatan, who was persuasive only because he was skilled at manipulating language and people. She was sure that had she the time to reflect on what he was saying she'd find plenty of flaws and fallacies.

Willis, on the other hand, was forming in his mind an image of a man who falls through the ice on a lake and finds himself standing waist deep in cold water. Every time he attempts to pull himself back up onto the ice shelf it gives way under his weight. Holt was, in a way, telling him that atheism is like that ice. It just can't support the weight he's asking it to bear. If Holt were to be believed only theism can sustain the weight of an objective morality.

The irony, Willis thought to himself, was that he often made a somewhat similar case to his students when teaching his literature classes. He'd tell them that we choose our own morality, our own values, that man was a morally autonomous Prometheus, but he always assumed without thinking much about it that the menu of moral options from which we choose consisted primarily of objective alternatives. It never really occurred to him that if atheism is true all our moral choices are in fact subjective and arbitrary, and if that's true there's no stopping point short of moral nihilism. If atheism is true and there's no life after death there really was no moral reason for Faustus to decline the devil's offer.

Willis couldn't bring himself to accept that when he judged someone to be a good or bad person he was really saying no more than that he liked or didn't like how the person acted, yet what more was he saying? He realized that many of the writers he'd read and taught to his students over the years had come to precisely the conclusion Holt was pressing upon him. He recalled specifically a passage from Tolstoy in which the great Russian author of *War and Peace* said:

The attempts to found a morality apart from religion are like the attempts of   children who, wishing to transplant a flower that pleases them, pluck it from the   roots that seem to them unpleasing and superfluous, and stick it rootless into the   ground. Without religion there can be no real, sincere morality, just as without   roots there can be no real flower.

He had always dismissed texts like this. He looked around, saw many people who believed as he did about God who nonetheless maintained high standards in their personal lives, and he just ignored, without thinking much about them, the contrary views of Tolstoy, *et al*. Holt, though, was holding the difficulty before him so insistently that he had to confront it. The preacher wasn't letting him ignore it.

"Modern secularists hold two mutually exclusive desires," Loren was saying. "They want to be free of God, and at the same time they want to make moral judgments. They want to talk about good and evil while discarding the only possible foundation for using moral language at all. They can't have it both ways. They want to say both that cruelty is wrong and that there is no God, but those two propositions can't both be true."

His voice was calm and winsome. There was nothing of the fanatic about him, nothing that was overly zealous, and the others were content to let him continue uninterrupted. Even Marie, who was quietly stewing, conceded Loren the floor as he tried to build his case.

"A pilot who finds himself flying in zero visibility with no instruments–no horizon, no GPS, nothing but his own intuition–has to fly 'by the seat of his pants,' by whatever feels best to him. Our culture is like that–flying by the seat of its pants, morally speaking, and that almost always results in vertigo and a death spiral."

Holt thought he'd already talked too much and was afraid he was boring Willis and his wife whom, he suspected, were only listening to him out of courtesy. He thought it time to bring the discussion, or at least his part of it, to a conclusion.

"I'm sure you're familiar with Hemmingway's aphorism, Willis, that, 'What's moral is what you feel good after, and what's immoral is what you feel bad after.' That pretty much sums up how a secular society has to think about right and wrong.

"Science can tell us how things work and technology makes life easier to live, but neither can tell us anything about how we *should* live. They don't tell us whether we should be kind or cruel, whether we should help the poor or let them fend for themselves, whether we should conserve the world's resources for future generations or squander them on ourselves. What could science have to say about any of this? It can tell us how to clone a human being but it has nothing to say about whether we should."

Like a lawyer resting his case, Holt leaned back in his chair, arched his eyebrows, as if to punctuate his last thought and drew the last sip of punch from his cup.

Willis had listened patiently and politely to Holt's disquisition, still convinced nonetheless that science had eliminated the need for God, but feeling less sure of it than he was two weeks ago. He was somewhat chagrined that it had never crossed his mind that rejecting belief in God meant embracing a view of morality that made right and wrong essentially meaningless terms. If atheism is true and if Holt was correct then morality was nothing more than an illusion created by our genes. It was a social fashion like the width of a tie or the cut of one's lapel, it's all just a matter of popular taste and approbation.

Maybe it was the influence of his early family life, maybe it was his genetics, but he was temperamentally averse to nihilism. Yet he had to concede, at least tentatively, that Holt was raising a serious practical problem for him: How is it rational for an atheist to make moral judgments about anyone else's behavior? Can an atheist such as himself speak of objective moral obligations and duties? What anchored moral judgments?

Willis had a fleeting picture of a man in a boat caught in a swift current. The man threw out the anchor, but it caught on the floating log of reason which did nothing to arrest the boat's drift. Then the man tried hooking the anchor to something inside the boat itself, but, of course, that was useless. If reason and internal feelings were inadequate anchor points, what could he fasten the boat to to keep it from drifting away?

Still, he was far from conceding that Holt was right and he was wrong, but demonstrating, even to his own satisfaction, that Holt's Christianity was factually vacuous, had proven more difficult than he'd anticipated. He wasn't sure what dredged up the words of Friedrich Nietzsche from his subconscious, but a statement by the 19th century philosopher flashed across his mind: "What decides against Christianity now," the great atheist once wrote, "is our taste, not our reasons." Was Nietzsche's rejection of Christian theism just a matter of personal taste? Was Willis'?

Willis decided to soldier on, probing Loren's defenses for a weakness he could exploit. Besides, he was certain Marie would be disappointed, to say the least, were he to retreat from the field at this point. He decided to launch one more sally.

"I guess I'd just repeat what I said earlier, Loren, science has demonstrated that we're just material beings, nothing more than atoms and energy. There's no soul, no spirit, nothing but a physical body with a physical brain that produces all of the phenomena we call mental events. And just as we're purely physical matter, so is everything else. There's nothing else. Nothing that can't be reduced to material 'stuff,' anyway. Physics fixes all the facts about reality."

Loren thought about that for a moment as he swept more cookie crumbs into a napkin. He looked at Willis and smiled. "I think that claim is self-refuting, Willis. It's claiming that physics determines what's true, but how could physics determine whether that claim itself is true? Besides, even if it *were* true it would just confirm what I've been saying, wouldn't it? How can atoms and energy impose or produce moral duties? If we're just material beings then morality really is a delusion. If matter is all there is then material things are all that matters. In fact, though, I doubt very much that we're just matter. I think it's very likely that we possess an immaterial mind or soul."

Willis was listening carefully for something he could leverage into rhetorical advantage. He couldn't imagine how Holt would support what he'd just said and was hoping for some blatant weakness in his reasons that he could refute in order to garner a few points and salvage some shred of honor from this discussion.

"I think you'd have a hard time demonstrating that, Pastor. We can trace all of our mental events to the functioning of our brains. The idea that we have something else, something immaterial like a mind, or soul as you call it, that plays a role, is a completely unnecessary hypothesis. What would this mind do that can't be explained by the brain?"

"The reason I think there's something fundamentally immaterial about us, Willis, is that sensations like seeing blue, or tasting something sweet, or feeling pain, can't be just physical, can they?"

"Sure they can," Willis replied, "those things are just nerves and sparks in the brain. That's all."

Loren shrugged. "I don't think so, Willis. Was the grief your brother and Patty endured while Alicia was missing just atoms bouncing around in their brains? If so, why pay that sensation any more attention than we'd pay to indigestion? How do atoms, physical matter, produce the sensation of grief, or pain, or blue? If you could walk around inside the brain of a giant while he was looking at the sky would you see blue in his brain anywhere? Where would 'sweet' be? Would you hear the music the brain was hearing? No, all you'd see are atoms interacting with other atoms, but the sensations he's experiencing are something else altogether, and there must be something else besides atoms and molecules at work in the brain that's responsible for them. After all, how could chemical reactions possibly produce a belief, or understanding, or create a doubt?"

Loren twiddled his empty paper cup in his fingers, and raised his eyes toward the others in a questioning look as if to tacitly invite an answer to his questions, but no answer was forthcoming.

"When you read a page in a book you're looking at chemicals on paper. That causes chemicals in your brain to jostle around and neurons to fire, but how does any of that produce the *meaning* you get from the page? Where does meaning come from? There's no meaning in atoms or sparks across nerves. Meaning is a product of conscious minds and minds aren't material. They're a different substance altogether.

"In fact, Willis, a lot of scientists are coming to the conclusion that so far from everything being made up of matter, matter itself is a made up of mind, or is at least a mental phenomenon. According to some physicists who study quantum mechanics immaterial consciousness is the ultimate reality."

Loren smiled, diffidently. "You know, Willis, I said a moment ago that if matter is all there is then material things are all that matters, but I bet you don't really think that material things are all that matters, and I'll bet you also think that the most important things in life aren't merely material either."

It was dawning on Willis that he'd completely underestimated Loren Holt. He expected that a Christian pastor would try to bury him under a pile of Bible verses and shallow theology, but that's not who Holt was at all. He'd chosen to engage Willis on his own turf, and his arguments had not only taken him by surprise, they were much more formidable than Willis had anticipated. Whether he was right or not, and Willis was convinced he just couldn't be, Holt was not the lightweight the college professor had assumed he'd be a week ago. Grudgingly, Willis could sense himself developing a growing respect for the pastor.

Loren, for his part, was actually a little ambivalent about the value of conversations like this. He enjoyed them, to be sure, but he was convinced that it was very difficult to persuade someone to accept a point of view to which they were viscerally opposed by means of arguments. No one is more difficult to persuade, no matter how strong the evidence or how good the argument with which he's presented, than the man who's already convinced that his partner in dialogue just has to be wrong.

Nor was Holt actually trying to persuade Willis of anything other than that Christian theism was a rational, coherent view of the world, perhaps more rational and coherent than any of its competitors, and that everyone should hope theism is true because if it's false human existence is little else than an absurd, tragic, and very bleak farce.

Loren saw exchanges such as he was engaging in with Willis Hoffmeyer as an important means of defending the rationality of his beliefs, and as such it was worthwhile, but as a means of actually changing minds, he doubted its efficacy. Despite the homage paid to reason, especially by skeptics like Willis and Marie, rationality isn't usually the deciding factor which determines whether people accept or reject a new belief, at least not beliefs about God. This state of affairs occasionally disappointed him. He thought it almost a perversity of human nature that appeals to the intellect were so often unconvincing, but he realized that he was just like everyone else in this regard. He knew from his own experience that unless the heart is persuaded first the mind never will be. He himself didn't come to God by way of an argument nor did most believers he knew.

Arguments may weaken a person's defenses but a mind can only be changed if first the heart is convinced.

Loren believed, too, that for many skeptics their atheism is a religion, though they often deny it, and as such it's often held with religious fervor. Many atheists bristle at this characterization and insist that atheism is *not* a religion, that it's simply the lack of a belief in God, but Loren was quite sure that it's more than that. He thought that the 19th century Russian writer Dostoyevsky offered a trenchant insight when he declared that people don't just *become* atheists, they *believe in* atheism. They embrace a creed that

affirms that nature is all there is, that the ultimate source of everything is impersonal, that everything reduces to matter and energy, and that there's no life beyond the grave. Atheism is not just the lack of belief in things like mind, soul, and God, it's the affirmative belief that the world does not include such things. If one's worldview contains beliefs about what's ultimately real and what isn't, then it is by its nature a religious affair since that's what religion is all about.

In any case, Loren was careful to present his case with humility and respect for Willis' objections. He was painfully aware that even if one were able to answer all of his opponent's arguments, though he may win his opponent's respect, and might even gain his agreement, he was just as likely to stoke his resentment. People do not always appreciate being shown that their most cherished convictions are not as compelling as they may have thought they were. Loren certainly didn't wish to provoke that kind of reaction in Willis or Marie.

Maybe the most effective way to break through to a man like Willis, Loren mused, was to show him that Christianity isn't merely creeds and rituals, it's ideally a way of life that radiates beauty. Loren was fond of Pope Benedict's claim that the best argument for the truth of Christianity is the beautiful lives it has produced and the beautiful art it has inspired. His own church hadn't produced much art, though they were working on it, but it was certainly producing some beautiful lives. Beauty, whether in nature, art, or in a human life, gives the beholder a glimpse of God, and that's what Loren wanted the Hoffmeyer's to experience. People who might otherwise never be open to the message of the gospel may be disarmed by an encounter with people trying to live the life prescribed by Christ. Maybe if he could show Willis and Marie what folks in his church actually do, how the gospel is actually lived out by people trying to be faithful to it, that might prove far more compelling than his decidedly unpersuasive philosophical appeals.

"But, look, this is all too somber a conversation for this happy occasion," Loren concluded as he stood to lock up the building and head home. "Why don't you both come by some morning next week. I'll show you around and you can see what we do here. I think you'd enjoy the tour."

Willis and Marie were non-committal, and Loren didn't really think they'd accept his invitation, but he hoped they would. He expected that if they did he might be able to plant at least a little doubt in their minds about the accuracy of their opinion of Christianity and Christians.

❦

Michael, Carlos, and Danny relaxed in the hotel lounge making small talk when one of them noticed a newsbreak on the television announcing that an Islamic terrorist group called Boko Haram had kidnapped several dozen young girls in Nigeria. The expectation was that the girls would be pressed into service as sex slaves. The same thing was happening in Iraq where Islamic radicals were seizing any non-Muslim girls they came across to be sold as slaves or to be forcibly wed to Muslim fighters.

"It's everywhere," Carlos mumbled to no one in particular. "For every one we rescue a hundred others are lost forever. It's pretty depressing."

"Maybe Luis was right," Danny commented sardonically, though he certainly didn't believe it.

"Who's Luis?" Michael inquired.

"He was the informant we had in Mexico," Carlos explained. "He and Danny had a debate about ethics, if you can believe it, just after I was supposed to have been butchered in the next room." Carlos was laughing at the mental image he was conjuring. "Anyway, Danny's been bothered by it ever since." Carlos was smiling at Danny who affected a look of *faux* irritation at being teased about the exchange he'd had with Luis.

"I didn't know what to say to the guy," Danny added. "He seemed pretty smart, actually, and he was saying that sex trafficking is just men doing what comes naturally. Preying on girls and all, isn't wrong, it's just survival of the fittest, or something."

"So that's why you said tonight that you guys should talk to the preacher," Michael said to Carlos.

"Yeah, if you're really bothered by what Luis told you I think we ought to go see the pastor, and see what he says, Danny. Maybe he'll have some answers for our Mexican friend. Can't hurt."

"Yeah, if you want, but I don't think he'd be much help," Danny replied, downing the last of the beer he'd been nursing. "He's just a preacher."

CHAPTER EIGHT

Saturday morning found Loren pecking away at his office computer working on a sermon appropriate to the events that had come so close to breaking the collective heart of a congregation which had agonized in empathy with the Hoffmeyer family during Alicia's disappearance.

His deliberations were interrupted by a light rap on his open door. Lifting his eyes from the monitor he saw Danny Howe peeking around the door frame. Loren was surprised and delighted at the same time. People say they'd like to get together, but it's often little more than a pleasantry. These two apparently meant it.

"Come in, come in," he urged. Danny entered the office followed by Carlos.

After handshakes, invitations to sit, orders for coffee, and solicitations about their well-being, Loren took a seat behind his desk. The two men from CSR sat down across from him. Carlos scanned the paintings on the wall and the shelves heavy with books.

"So, what brings you guys here this morning?" Loren wondered.

"Well," Carlos began rather cryptically, "we were talking about things, we had nothing else to do, so we decided to take you up on your invitation last night to visit."

Loren smiled. "What sorts of things were you talking about?"

Danny picked up for Carlos while his friend studied a large framed print of William Holman Hunt's *Light of the World* hanging on the wall above Loren's head.

"I've been a little bothered by something a guy we ran into in Mexico said." Danny was referring obliquely to Luis whom he had threatened, so to speak, with torture and who retaliated by torturing Danny with a baffling dialogue on metaphysics. "I can't get it out of my head, I don't know why, but anyway we thought you might be a good person to talk to about it." It would've been more accurate to say that *Carlos* thought Holt might be a good person to talk to about Danny's concerns because Danny didn't think the pastor would have much to offer at all.

Loren leaned back in his chair, feeling flattered and somewhat ashamed of himself for feeling that way. "What did he say?"

"He asked me if I believed in God. I told him 'no' because I don't think I do, but I don't really know, and he said that then I have to agree with him that we're just animals in the jungle, and there's really nothing wrong with trafficking kids. Or something like that."

Loren gazed at him without responding. Danny was obviously disturbed by what he'd been told. It was difficult for him to believe that if he didn't believe in God he had to conclude that there wasn't anything wrong with trafficking kids. He returned Holt's gaze with the mild hope that Loren might surprise him with some helpful counsel. Carlos shifted his eyes from the painting to Loren in anticipation of his response.

"What do you think I should have told him? Aren't we different from animals because we can talk and use our brains?" By this Loren assumed Danny meant that humans are rational.

"I mean, doesn't that make us special? Anyway, me and Carlos were talking about this and we thought we'd stop by and see what you said about it."

Loren was a little dumbfounded by the sudden appearance of these men in his office. These were men who'd seen and done so much in their lives, these were men who in his mind were genuine heroes, and they were looking to him, who had done so little, at least in his own estimation, for answers to a question of apparently crucial importance to them. He was mildly perplexed by the incongruity of it.

"Well, Danny, if you want me to say that what that man told you is wrong you might be asking the wrong guy." Loren smiled and stirred his coffee.

Danny looked a bit surprised and a little disappointed.

"The reason I say that," Loren went on, "is because things like language and intelligence make us unique in the animal kingdom, but we're still just animals. After all, bats are unique animals, too, but they're still just animals. Same with birds, and fish that can sense electric fields, they're all unique in their own ways, but they're still just animals. And the fella' who told you that we're just animals was right, I think, if there is no God."

This was neither the answer Danny wanted nor expected. He anticipated that a preacher would assure him that human beings were of loftier station, that we were more than animals, that it was wrong to buy and sell kids whether God existed or not, and he was some-what confused that that wasn't what Pastor Holt was telling him.

"So, if we're just animals trafficking kids isn't wrong?" Danny's voice had an edge to it.

"I didn't quite say that," Loren replied, "but it's very hard to say *why* it's wrong unless there's a God. In my view abusing children is terribly wrong, but I say that because I believe we're created in the image of God, and he loves us, and nobody has the right to harm what God loves. Because we're created in his image and because he loves us we have dignity, worth, and human rights, but take God out of that mix and all of those things collapse. God's the only thing that can provide an adequate foundation for them. Unless human rights come from God they're just comfortable fictions we tell ourselves.

"If you believe that what those men in Mexico were doing is evil, and it is, then I urge you to reconsider your answer to the man's question about whether you believe in God, Danny."

This was more reassuring to Danny, but he was still a little uneasy. He didn't like the implication that if he insisted on believing that God *didn't* exist he really had no reason to disagree with Luis.

"Couldn't we just have a sense of right and wrong as part of being human?" Danny countered. "Maybe we just have it from nature."

Loren steepled his fingers under his chin as he considered how best to answer Danny's objection.

"Sure, I guess so, but if nature's the source of our sense of right and wrong there's no reason why we should pay any attention to it. A moral sentiment like kindness, if it results from a blind, purposeless process like evolution, is no more obligatory than is the desire to be selfish which also comes from the same process."

Danny was thinking back to how Luis used the idea that we're just a product of nature to justify his own occupational interests.

"Impersonal causes can't impose moral obligations," Loren continued. To think they can is like saying that something like gravity can impose a duty to be honest.

"We can only have a duty to be kind, or to respect the humanity of others, if that duty is imposed intentionally by a conscious, personal being which is itself perfectly good and capable of holding us accountable. That's why I think you should reconsider what you believe about God."

Loren took a sip of coffee while looking across the rim of his mug at the two men. They were listening intently to him which intrigued him since usually when he talked philosophically people's eyes glazed over. He was also amazed that the conversation was so similar to the discussion he'd had with Willis and Marie the previous evening. He

probably hadn't had this conversation more than once or twice in the last five years, and now he was having it twice within the space of about twelve hours.

Since there was silence in the office Loren continued his thought.

"Most of us do have a powerful intuition that some things are just wrong. I think that intuition is a pointer to God. It's his way of grabbing us by the shoulders and saying, 'Don't you see? Don't you see that a moral law must have a Source?' If there's no God then that strong moral intuition is like a wisdom tooth–you have it, but you don't really need it. It just gets in the way."

Notwithstanding his interest in the art adorning Holt's office Carlos had been listening carefully to the conversation and chose this moment to speak up.

"I was on a rescue once in Dubai." Loren could discern a slight Hispanic inflection in his words. "A wealthy sheik had a house full of children, some of whom he'd bought from their parents and some from traders like the people who took Alicia to Mexico."

He held his coffee mug in both hands and stared at Loren's desk in front of him. He raised his dark eyes to meet Loren's.

"The way he treated those kids was so cruel it's hard to put into words. They weren't allowed to sleep in the house, they had to sleep in the barn with the horses. They were forced to work on his estate from before sunup to after sundown in scorching heat, with little water, only one meal. It was awful. Girls and boys. He used them as slave labor and sex toys. He was big into child porn and would have parties where he'd film his guests sexually abusing these kids."

Loren sat silently, but anger began to churn inside him as he listened to Carlos' story. He was not naïve, but he always wanted to disbelieve stories of human depravity. He just didn't want to think that human beings could be so diabolically evil, but, of course, he knew they often were. He knew they were sometimes worse than he could even imagine.

"One boy tried to run away, but the sheik's thugs caught him. He was about thirteen years old. The sheik made all the kids come out to his garden to watch the punishment. See, he was very rich and one of his hobbies was keeping tigers in a big fenced in pen like at a zoo in his garden. He had the boy placed in the pen at feeding time. He told him that, if, at the end of fifteen minutes, he was still alive then he was free to go. The boy was terrified, shaking and hysterical. He knew he couldn't avoid hungry tigers for that long."

Carlos' eyes homed in on Loren's as though he were trying to see straight into Loren's mind.

"The sheik and his friends laughed as the tigers ripped the boy apart while the other kids were forced to watch, I suppose as a lesson on what happens to kids who try to escape. I know all this 'cause the kids we extracted from that place told us. That was just one of the stories they told us of the hell they went through.

138

"So," Carlos concluded, "I guess what I'm asking is, are you saying that someone has to believe in God in order to believe that what was done to that boy was evil?"

Loren didn't speak. To do so would've seemed unforgivably glib. A line from Edmund Burke flashed through his mind: "There's no safety for honest men but by believing all possible evil of evil men." As much as he wanted to think better of people he knew it was very hard to overestimate the wickedness of which some human beings were capable. There seemed to be no limit to man's iniquity and cruelty.

When after a few moments he was able to put the story far enough out of his mind to gather his thoughts he offered his response. "No, not exactly, Carlos. One can *believe* something is a great evil even if one doesn't believe in God, but what I'm saying is that if the atheist is right about God then the belief that something actually*is* evil is mistaken. Unless there's a God there are no grounds for saying that what that sheik did was wrong. In a Godless universe no one has an objective duty to refrain from cruelty or any other behavior. In the world of the atheist's imagining might makes right. If you've got the power you can do whatever you want. If there are no eternal consequences then the word 'wrong,' at least in a moral context, doesn't have much meaning."

Holt set his mug down on his desk and crossed his legs.

"When we no longer believe in God we'll soon believe we're just animals," Loren looked at Danny as he spoke. "And when we believe we're just animals we'll soon behave like animals, and, objectively speaking, if God doesn't exist what that sheik did to that boy is essentially no different nor more wrong than what the tiger did to him."

Holt sighed deeply and related an episode he'd witnessed a couple of months previous. He was walking downtown and happened to look up to see a magnificent falcon swooping and swerving between the tall office buildings. Half a block further on he saw the bird again, now higher in the sky. Suddenly, it folded its wings and dove at incredible speed directly toward a pigeon gliding over the street. The falcon's talons struck the pigeon with such force that a spray of feathers exploded from the bird. Mortally wounded by the strike, the hapless pigeon fluttered helplessly to the ground and died. The falcon just flew off. It wasn't even interested in eating its victim. It apparently killed it just to amuse itself.

"The falcon wasn't evil," Loren emphasized. "It was just doing what falcons do. Killing is no more wrong for us than it is for the falcon unless we're obligated by a personal moral authority to refrain from killing. If we're convinced that it's wrong to harm innocent children then we're tacitly admitting that that authority exists."

"That's hard to accept, Pastor." Danny objected. "Feeding that boy to tigers was wrong whether there's a God or not."

Loren said nothing. He hadn't been able to persuade Willis and his wife last night, and he didn't seem to fare any better with Carlos or Danny today. One part of his brain told him he had a "knockdown" argument for the necessity of God's existence, at least for anyone who wanted to believe in right and wrong, and another part was telling him that there really was no such thing as a knockdown argument for anything having to do with God.

He'd read somewhere once that when people were given a choice between accepting the existence of God or abandoning belief that there are objective moral duties, many people would sooner abandon belief in objective moral duties and embrace moral nihilism than accept the existence of God. At least Danny wasn't making that move. As far as he could *tell* he wasn't, anyway.

"There's one more thing I might say about this." Loren took a sip of coffee and set the cup down on his desk. "All of us are outraged at the evil Carlos described, but moral outrage only makes sense if the world could have been other than the way it is. Given atheism, though, and given the laws of nature, the world is the only way it could have been. Both the Christian and the atheist can say that they wish the world were different, but only the Christian can say that it *should* be different. If atheism is true the world is as it must be. That's pretty depressing."

Loren smiled and let the matter drop, and the conversation shifted to other topics. In response to Loren's query Danny gave a very vague outline of how they'd managed to rescue Alicia, withholding the more uncomfortable details. Eventually the men rose to leave. The pastor had the sinking feeling that they were a little dissatisfied with the outcome of their visit, but he didn't know what else he could have said.

As the three men stood near the door saying their goodbyes Carlos' eye caught a poem on the wall which he began to read. "What's this?" he asked Loren as he pointed to the poem.

"That's a poem by a 19th century poet named Francis Thompson," Loren replied. "It's called *The Hound of Heaven*." Loren stepped over to where Carlos was standing and explained that it was about a man trying to flee from God who is relentlessly pursuing him. God loves the man too much to let him get away without a chase.

"So God's the hound," Carlos commented.

"Yes." Loren divulged that a lot of people, himself included, find the poem to be deeply poignant because it describes so beautifully

their own experience. The first twenty lines were especially meaningful to him. He began to read them slowly and softly:

> I fled Him, down the nights and down the days;
> I fled Him, down the arches of the years;
> I fled Him, down the labyrinthine ways
> Of my own mind; and in the mist of tears
> I hid from Him, and under running laughter.
> Up vistaed hopes I sped;
> And shot, precipitated,
> Adown Titanic glooms of chasmèd fears,
> From those strong Feet that followed, followed after.
> But with unhurrying chase,
> And unperturbèd pace,
> Deliberate speed, majestic instancy,
> They beat—and a Voice beat
> More instant than the Feet—
> 'All things betray thee, who betrayest Me.'
> I pleaded, outlaw-wise,
> By many a hearted casement, curtained red,
> Trellised with intertwining charities;
> (For, though I knew His love Who followèd,
> Yet was I sore adread
> Lest, having Him, I must have naught beside).

"I especially like that last line," Loren admitted. "It captures the
fear that so many people have that if they submit to God they won't
be able to have anything else they enjoy."

Loren let his words sink in as Carlos continued to read the rest of the poem. When he'd finished he turned to Loren with a smile and a soft "*hmm*" of approval.

The men were ready to leave.

"By the way, I'd love to hear sometime how you liberated those children from that sheik in Dubai," Loren said as he shook Carlos' hand. "Maybe we can talk about it sometime."

Carlos smiled. "Maybe," he replied vaguely and then added somewhat out of the blue that he often wished that he'd followed his youthful desire to enter the priesthood. He had a great deal of respect for the priests he had known and for everyone who chooses the life of a servant of God and man.

"It's not too late, Carlos," Holt rejoined. "I'm sure you'd make a fine priest."

"And," he said to Danny as he clasped his hand, "I hope you'll think more about what we talked about today."

He gave them his cell number in case they ever wanted to get in touch with him. The two men thanked him, and Loren said a silent prayer for them as he watched them walk out of his office and down the hall.

❧

Once Carlos and Danny had departed, Loren returned to his sermon for the next day. He wanted to tie it in somehow to the story of Alicia's rescue since that had been foremost in the minds and prayers of his congregation that week, but for some reason, despite the fascinating drama he had to draw on for material, ideas on how to work it into a sermon just wouldn't come to him, at least not in any coherent fashion.

His mind kept wandering. It went from trying to imagine the horror of the boy in Carlos' story, which he was able to push out of his mind only with difficulty, to thinking about what he could have said to Danny, to reflecting on the poem on his wall, to reminiscing about the path that had led him from his years as a college student to this time and place.

The men he'd just been talking with were willing to risk their lives to save children they didn't even know from a life of abject degradation. Sometimes, Loren knew, the children they rescue don't want to be rescued. Sometimes they've been sold into slavery by their own parents and have nowhere to go once they're freed. Despite these frustrations these men still lay their own lives on the line to save them or at least give them the opportunity for a better life.

They asked nothing for themselves. Not even thanks. He couldn't help asking himself what *he* was risking. How does what he's doing with his life measure up to what they're doing, he wondered. He hoped he and his church were doing a lot of good for people, but he wasn't really risking anything, certainly not his life. The comparison to those who were made him once again feel inadequate.

His mind dredged up bitter memories of his dissipated, self-absorbed college years. Recalling some of the things he did as a younger man brought on literal shudders of shame and remorse, and he forced himself to put thoughts of his college years out of his mind. They were just too unpleasant to dwell upon. In fact, his past was so full of such uncomfortable memories, such guilt, that reflecting on his youth was something he rarely did, and he wondered how many others were as haunted by their past as was he.

As a college freshman he'd been seduced by writers like Friedrich Nietzsche who convinced him that he, too, was a moral "overman" who stood above the common herd and was exempt from the bourgeois standards of behavior to which the mass of students with which he found himself surrounded paid lip service. He was beyond the categories of good and evil and the "slave morality" taken for granted by the mindless, inferior run of people. He set his own standards which, conveniently, were pretty low, and based primarily on a callow narcissism and egoism. He lived entirely for himself and treated with contempt anyone he regarded as an impediment to getting what he wanted. He used people like one uses a paper cup, discarding them when they were no longer useful to him. Anyone he couldn't dominate or bend to his will he eventually alienated and shunned.

Inevitably, whatever companions he had managed to acquire found him insufferable and gradually drifted away. Not willing to blame himself for their defection, he condemned them for their disloyalty. He was dabbling in drugs, drinking too much, wasting his leisure hours doing little of anything, and making a wreck of his health.

By the time he was a senior he was a social isolate, friendless, lonely, and living by himself. Throughout college he'd had a series of girlfriends, but in each case the relationship was shallow and ephemeral, based on physical attraction and usually ending in an angry quarrel. His parents could scarcely talk to him and were deeply concerned that he was on the verge of a breakdown. They were correct in their diagnosis, but the breakdown for which he was headed wasn't the kind they'd feared.

He eventually reached a place where he at last faced the fact that his life was imploding and would in due course become a complete ruin. He didn't want to continue in the direction he was headed, he was aware that he had for three years been morphing into something ugly, but the superficial allurements of life as he was living it seemed tantalizingly irresistible, so he continued almost helplessly on the heading he'd set for himself and continued, too, like a passive spectator, to watch his life unravel. He was dissolute, despondent, and gravitating inexorably toward personal disaster. He knew he had to stop, he had to gain control, but he couldn't, or, at any rate, wouldn't.

Despite all this he managed somehow, to this day he didn't know how, to keep his grades up. He read widely in literature and philosophy and was particularly attracted to the work of those writers who espoused an atheistic and/or nihilistic view of life, a worldview congenial to his own impulses, appetites and predilections. He recalled reading a line from Sigmund Freud who wrote that, "The moment a man questions the meaning and value of life he is sick since objectively neither has any existence." If that were true, he said to himself, why not just live however he wanted to live?

Then in the winter of his senior year his life changed radically and forever. The catalyst was a book written some 1600 years earlier. Loren was reading Augustine's *Confessions* for an elective literature class he was taking in his last semester. He'd never heard of Augustine before being assigned the work, but reading it was the most captivating, most exhilarating experience any book had ever afforded him.

He sat down with it in his cloistered apartment, and there on the first page were words that sprung off the paper at him. It was as if in opening the book he'd released a voice which spoke directly to him: "You have made us for yourself, O Lord, and our hearts are restless until they rest in you."

"Restless" was a perfect summation of everything he'd felt for the last four years, a succinct description of the turbulence and turmoil of his life. He read on and came to a description Augustine gives of himself that almost took his breath away:

I became evil for no reason. I had no motive for my wicked-ness except wickedness itself. It was foul, and I loved it. I loved the self-destruction, I loved my fall, not the object for which I had fallen but my fall itself. My depraved soul leaped down from your [God's] firmament to ruin. I was seeking not to gain anything by shameful means, but shame for its own sake.

He was stunned. It was as if Augustine were describing *him*. More than that, he had the sense that God was speaking to him through Augustine. He had rejected God as the fantasy of childish minds, but he was drawn to Augustine's meditations on God all the same. He continued to read the book every spare minute, over meals, while waiting for other classes to start, in the evenings. He put it down only with reluctance and was eager to take it up again whenever he could. When at last he came to Augustine's description of his conversion Loren broke down and wept. Without realizing it, Augustine's experience was what he had desired for himself for at least the past year, maybe longer.

That night he dreamt the most vivid, coherent dream he'd ever had. In it he saw himself stumbling recklessly into a pit of quicksand. Slowly, he began to sink. He panicked and thrashed about, flailing vainly for something to grasp hold of. Seized by terror as he felt himself sinking deeper, he realized he was completely helpless, he was unable to escape the pull of the muck that was sucking him under. Then at the last instant before his head was submerged he heard a voice saying, "Reach up, Loren, and take my hand."

At that moment he comprehended for the first time that he'd been hearing that voice his whole life but had persistently ignored it, resisted it, repressed it. Now in desperation he groped for the proffered hand. His hand brushed an arm, but his fingers were too slippery, the arm was too thickly muscled, and he couldn't hold onto it. His head slipped under, he felt himself suffocating, but at that instant a powerful grip locked onto his upraised arm and lifted him effortlessly up out of the mire. The next moment he lay prostrate on solid ground, exhausted, panting for breath. He looked around to see who had saved him, but there was no one. Even so, he knew.

He bolted awake from his dream and sat upright in his bed. Turning on the light he took the *Confessions* from the night table, opened it to Augustine's description of his conversion, and reread it, slowly digesting every word. When he finished he gently closed the book, lay quietly in his bed for a minute lost in thought, and then surrendered himself completely to the same Christ that had so radically changed the life of Augustine and many millions of others.

Even after his Augustinian moment it took years of slow growth with many stumbles and falls for him to even approach being the man he thought God wanted him to be, but his orientation was now completely different. His life's journey was now taking him in a direction precisely opposite to the course he had been following. The man he eventually became was very far from the man he had been becoming.

After graduation he felt impelled to somehow make up for the selfishness and indifference with which he had treated people. Apologies played an important role, but they weren't sufficient. He had a deep desire to do more, to do something which involved self-abnegation, something that would be the very opposite of the egoism and pride which had shaped his *persona* up until his encounter with

Augustine's Christ. The past was past, and he couldn't undo it, but he was resolved to make the future an atonement, somehow, for the past.

Through a series of fortuitous events he was introduced to a missionary who worked with indigenous Indians in eastern Panama. These people still lived in raised pole, open-air, thatched-roofed huts in the tropical forests much as had their ancestors. The missionary lived with them, teaching their children, providing them medical aid and working to develop reliable supplies of clean water. He agreed to mentor Holt, to take him on as an apprentice. His parents scarcely understood what their son was going through, why he would want to live in the jungle, or what accounted for the change in him, despite his attempts to explain it to them. Nevertheless, they were overjoyed to see him genuinely happy for the first time in a decade.

About four miles from the village which became his home there was a nature lodge that catered to European and North American eco-tourists. A number of the men in the village were employed at the lodge as maintenance workers, and every day they would set out on foot at 4:00 in the morning, walking a dirt road and traversing by raft a muddy river that was often swollen from rains. It was a strenuous three mile hike to the hard road and then another mile, with several precipitously steep slopes, on the other side of the hard road to the lodge. Arriving by 6:00 they would work all day in the oppressive tropical sun and then make the return trip in the evening. By the time they arrived back at their village they were exhausted and barely had time to eat and sleep before they were up again the next morning to do it all over again.

Loren made the trek with these men almost every day for the three years he lived among them—except when laid low by malaria or intestinal parasites—sweltering in the sun, mowing, painting, and gardening to keep the lodge and its grounds looking attractive for its clients. Their days were grueling, but none of the men ever complained. Loren was occasionally tempted to gripe, but he didn't yield to the urge, partly because the arduous life was for him a kind of penance, partly because he knew if he did complain it would diminish him in the eyes of the other men, and partly because, unlike his companions, Holt had another motive besides a meager pay to spur him to make the journey every day. On staff at the lodge was a young American naturalist whose job it was to lead tours through the jungle pointing out the monkeys, sloths, birds and other flora and fauna that inhabited the forests.

Her name was Olivia Harris, and Holt was bewitched the moment his eyes first fell upon her. She was just out of college, very intelligent, physically attractive, and the possessor of a voluminous knowledge of, and a profound love for, the natural history of the region.

Loren and Olivia began to see each other as their schedules permitted. Lunch breaks and evenings were spent in walks together around the grounds. In the fullness of time, they chose to marry, move back to the states, and start a family.

It was difficult for both of them to leave the people and the jungle that they'd come to love, but Loren had decided he wanted to go to seminary and eventually build an urban ministry, and Olivia supported his decision, albeit with some trepidation. For a girl with a passion for the natural beauty and rhythms of the tropics, being a pastor's wife, especially in an urban setting, would be a considerable adjustment, not one that would come easily to her.

Loren promised her that every year they'd take a vacation to Panama, and he faithfully kept that promise. Even so, their marriage suffered some very rocky early years during which it wasn't clear to either of them that it would hold together, but they were both committed to making it work, and so it did.

In seminary Loren read extensively in philosophy, theology and literature and people who had known him in his undergraduate years were dumbfounded by what they saw in him when they met him now. It was an astonishing transformation which he cheerfully attributed to an amazing grace.

Eventually he graduated from seminary, and after a brief stint as an associate pastor he and Olivia set out on their own to build a ministry in the church they currently served in Baltimore. That was some twenty years ago.

Now he sat at his computer trying to clear his mind of his conversation with Danny and Carlos and of the obtrusive details of his past which kept disrupting his concentration so that he could focus on writing his sermon. He knew the ideas would come to him soon enough. They usually did.

CHAPTER NINE

T he following Monday morning Loren was scheduled to meet with an HVAC crew to check the church's erratic heating system. He was leading some maintenance personnel into the bowels of the building when he received a call from his secretary telling him that Caleb Hoffmeyer and his brother were waiting for him in his office.

As soon as he was able to disengage from the HVAC inspection a very surprised Pastor Holt hurried to his office to greet the Hoffmeyer brothers. He was as pleased to hear that they were there as he was amazed that Willis had decided to come after all.

He found Caleb seated in a chair and Willis perusing the shelves of books that covered one wall of the office. His eyes settled on the painting which graced the wall behind Loren's chair. He continued to study it while his brother explained their presence there.

"Willis had some time this morning before his afternoon classes so he agreed to have a look at our ministry here." Caleb declared. He didn't mention that it took some sibling arm-twisting to get Willis to agree to the visit. Marie had other engagements which afforded her an excuse not to participate.

"Well, I'm delighted you could stop in," was Loren's understated reply. Let me pour you both some coffee, and we'll take a walk around. The place is pretty busy here on Monday mornings."

The two men accepted the offer, and Loren retrieved three mugs from a shelf above his desk. He prepared the coffee to each man's taste while Willis, standing in front of the painting with his hands clasped behind his back, continued to examine the work.

"Can you tell me a little bit about this painting, Loren?"

"Yes, the original was done by Holman Hunt in the early 1850s. It's called *The Light of the World*, and as you can see it shows Christ holding a lantern outside what appears to be a rural cottage. The background is in late twilight, and the foreground is illuminated by the lantern. Christ is knocking on a door overgrown with weeds suggesting that it's never been opened. Hunt once said that the door represents the 'obstinately shut mind.' Notice that there's no handle or latch on the outside of the door. It can only be opened from the inside.

"The painting is a riff on the Biblical passage in which Jesus says 'Behold, I stand at the door and knock. If anyone hears my voice and opens the door, I will come in to him, and dine with him, and he with me.' He's apparently not getting much of a welcome at the door in the painting."

"That's Revelation 3:20, isn't it?" Caleb asked.

"Yes, it is," his pastor affirmed. "It's a very lovely piece of art, don't you think? Richly symbolic."

Loren portioned out the coffee, and the three men set off to survey what he and his congregation had built in the twenty-odd years of his tenure there.

The church building itself was a grand old granite structure formerly owned by Episcopalians, but as the neighborhood declined the original membership shrank until finally the previous occupants sold the building to Loren's rapidly growing non-denominational congregation. Under his leadership the church had expanded steadily over the years and boasted an interesting ethnic mix of blacks, whites, Hispanics, Asians and some who were a little bit of all of them.

On one side of the church building sat the parsonage, where Loren and his wife lived and where they had raised three children, all of whom were now grown and fledged. On the other side was a former automobile dealership. The building had been purchased by the church and converted into the school that Loren and Olivia settled upon the night he'd been mugged. The capacious wrap-around parking lot, which once sported hundreds of new and used cars on display, now provided convenient parking for church services.

Loren conducted his guest and Caleb downstairs to a cafeteria. A kitchen on one side was bustling with people preparing soup and sandwiches for dozens of residents of the surrounding neighborhoods, many of them homeless alcoholics and/or drug addicts, who didn't qualify for much public assistance and who, in any case, weren't likely to spend what money they had on food.

"We open this up for a noon meal every day except Sunday. For some of the people who'll show up it'll be the only meal they'll have today. In the winter we put cots in here and use it for a shelter, especially when it's cold. The kitchen workers are all volunteers from the congregation, but we have a staff person whose job it is to get those people help with their addictions, or to find work, or whatever their biggest material need is."

One of the women was working close to where Loren stood, and he introduced her.

"This is Doris Weyland. She's an angel. She's pretty much run our lunch program, and a bunch of other things, for the last couple of years." Doris smiled, blushing with mild embarrassment at the praise.

"How's your son doing, Doris?" Pastor Holt inquired.

"He's coming to visit in a couple of weeks," Doris beamed after assuring Caleb that she'd been praying for Alicia and was so happy that his daughter was home safely. "He said he'd come to church with me. He also said he hopes to get a chance to see you."

"That's wonderful," Loren replied. Tell him I'm looking forward to seeing him again."

"I don't imagine her job's very easy," Willis opined, as the men moved on.

"No, it's not. Doris lost her husband Joe a few years ago, and she's pretty much made service to others her life's work ever since. She's been a wonderful asset to our ministry here. Her son teaches history at Adams State. We met a few years ago when her husband passed away.

"Come on. Let's go over to the school."

Loren led them through the door of the old auto showroom. There were kids everywhere. "This is our daycare. We operate it primarily for single moms who work, but anyone can bring their children here. The cost is reduced ten percent every Sunday the mom is in church, up to forty percent for the month. Single working moms can bring their kids here for free if they attend the Bible studies or the parenting and financial management classes we offer."

"Sounds like bribery," Willis noted wryly.

"It is," Loren confessed with a smile, "and it works pretty well."

"Who runs it?"

"We have two full-time staffers, two part-timers, and a bunch of volunteers. We ask the moms to help out several days a month. I'm lucky to have a lot of good people on staff and some wonderful volunteers, like Caleb and Patty, to help out. We couldn't begin to do all this without them. Let's go this way."

The route took them by the old automobile service department where cars had formerly been repaired. The area had been converted into a small gym, and several kids were playing basketball and ping-pong.

"Hey," Loren chided, "aren't you guys supposed to be in class?"

"We have a study hall, Reverend," was the reply.

"What're you studying with that basketball?"

"How to get rich in the NBA," the young man quipped with a grin. Loren and his companions laughed.

"I want to show you something over there." He nodded in the direction of a hallway that led to a half dozen rooms that had been partitioned off from the old service bays. They were roomy enough to accommodate twelve to fifteen students each.

"We added a grade to our school each year for the first seven years we were in operation. We started with kindergarten and built up to sixth grade, which is where we originally planned to stop, but after a couple of years we decided we had to add grades all the way through high school. Once our kids had completed sixth grade we had to pass them off to the public school system which broke our hearts. The public schools are so hamstrung by legalities, regulations, and political correctness that they have a hard time teaching kids what's really important. They have difficulty teaching kids how to be good men and women. They can tell kids it's wrong to cheat on their work, but they can't tell them *why* it's wrong. If you can't give kids reasons *why* something's wrong you're not likely to persuade them that it *is* wrong. So, we just decided that we needed to keep the kids until they graduated.

"We also use some rooms over in the church. We've got a lot more applicants than we have room for, and we're wrestling with what to do about it. It's a good problem to have, I guess."

"Where do you get your teachers?" Willis asked.

"All the classroom teachers and our headmaster are state certified. We can't pay them as much as they'd make in the public schools in the city, but the working conditions here are pretty good. There are plenty of teachers out there looking for jobs so we haven't had too much trouble filling slots with good people. We get a lot of kids whose parents want to send them to private schools but can't afford it. We work with them on the tuition which is pretty low anyway."

Willis was impressed by the kids who were passing him in the hall. "Are they all required to dress up?"

"Yeah. Kids' performance and behavior tends to track their dress. When you dress well you perform better. Everybody knows it, but for some reason we don't let our public schools take advantage of it."

"How do you respond to the objection that uniformity stifles individualism and creativity?" Willis inquired.

Loren shrugged his shoulders as if to say that that wasn't an objection he heard very often, if at all.

"All their favorite sports stars wear uniforms," Loren answered, "and a lot of kids wear their heroes' jerseys outside of school. Many of them have pictures at home of older siblings who serve in the military. They're extremely proud of their brothers and sisters and how they look in their uniforms. Why should it be any different at school? We try to teach kids to take pride in their appearance just like their brothers and sisters in the military do. Nobody has ever objected that I can remember."

Apparently it was time for recess and younger children were filling up the hallway. Loren directed the group back toward the gym. As they walked they were continually stopped by people offering Caleb their heartfelt expressions of joy that Alicia was home. Between these interludes Loren tried to explain another facet of the church's ministry.

"We have several physicians in the congregation, as well as a couple of physician's assistants, a nurse practitioner, and several RNs. Most of them volunteer their time to come in here and help our kids stay healthy. It's free and some of the parents would rather use this service than use the Medicaid system, especially since some doctors no longer accept Medicaid patients.

"The medical folks usually come in on Saturdays to check the kids, give shots, write prescriptions, that sort of thing. They carve out a couple of weeks from their practices each summer to go on a medical mission to Haiti or Africa. They're amazing people. I wish we had more like them. We're also teaming with some other churches to develop a drug rehab program, but that's still in the works. We're thinking about what we can do to help children who are in this country illegally. It's not their fault that they're here, and we can't just pretend they're not.

"I should mention, too, a group of urban pastors who meet once a month with city officials. We invite these folks to tell us what problems they're facing that they just can't seem to solve, and we pray with them and for them. They're usually very grateful. Let's head back over to the church."

Willis was moved. "This is all pretty impressive that so many people feel such a desire to help people," he commented, "but you don't need to believe in God to do all this, do you? I mean, surely there are a lot of people who do this sort of work from secular motivations."

Willis didn't intend to sound contentious, at least not consciously. He was merely trying to reassure himself that the people in Loren's church were not unique just because they were Christians. He wanted to believe that one could do acts of charity and compassion quite apart from any motivation grounded in religious beliefs.

Loren, however, thought the question a bit gratuitous and didn't respond at first. He just walked along with his eyes on the ground. After a few steps he answered. "Maybe not, Willis. Anyone could pitch in to help meet the needs this city has. All I can tell you is that the people in this church, and others around the city who are doing this kind of work, often wish they had more company."

Willis' next question was perhaps even more clumsy.

"But why do *you* do it, Loren? Are you afraid of missing out on heaven if you don't?" It sounded snarkier than Willis intended. He wasn't trying to goad Holt. On the contrary, he was genuinely interested in plumbing his motives, but it sounded to Loren like condescension, almost as if Willis were being sarcastic.

It sounded that way to Caleb, too, who snapped his head around to glare at his brother as if to ask him how he could be so rude. He sarcastically apologized to Loren for his brother's bad manners.

Willis realized his *faux pas* and apologized himself, trying to explain what he really meant, but Loren insisted that he took no offense, though that wasn't quite true. Nevertheless, taking offense would neither open Willis' heart nor his mind to what Loren wanted him to see. Instead he patiently tried to explain what he saw as the motivation for doing what he and others were doing, albeit in different ways in different settings all around the globe.

"Hope for heaven is hardly what motivates most Christians, Willis. They're not motivated by the hope of gaining what they know they already have. They're motivated instead by gratitude for having had it given them. Gratitude for what Jesus Christ did on the cross for each of us, including you, is what makes people here eager to volunteer their time and money to help others make their own lives better, both spiritually and materially.

"God could certainly do this without us, but he wants us to do it. It's good for these people and good for us, too. It makes us grow."

Holt believed that he himself was a man who'd been done a great kindness and had spent the last couple of decades of his life trying to give something in return to his Benefactor, realizing all along that there's nothing he could do that would begin to repay the grace he'd been shown.

Once while engaged in compiling a collection of his sermons into a book he hoped to publish he was reminded of a present his son had given Olivia when the boy was about five years old. It was a bracelet made of beads he'd fashioned in his kindergarten class. He'd put more than a little effort and care into crafting the gift, and was eager to see his mother's face light up with joy when he offered it to her. He wanted to do something to show his love and appreciation for his mom. When he presented her with his bracelet Olivia accepted it with lots of hugs and kisses, delighted much more by the motivation behind the gift than with the gift itself. Loren felt the same way about his book back then and his ministry to the city's poor now. They were, in a sense, humble gifts. He hoped God would be delighted with his efforts though he knew God could have managed perfectly well in Baltimore had Holt stayed in Panama for the rest of his life.

"We do this because we believe this is what God wants us to do, Willis. We believe that we're his physical hands in this community. He works through us and wants us to love these people because he loves them. It's pretty simple, really. Dietrich Bonhoeffer said that the church is the church only when it exists for others. We're trying to be the church."

"The task must at times seem Sisyphean. So many of these people have so little. The problems in poor communities like this seem so deep and intractable, don't they?" Willis mumbled all this to his brother, who, despite his and Patty's integral involvement in the social ministry of the church, had remained quiet and let Loren do the talking. Now in response to his brother's remark he spoke as they walked.

"Americans, even poor Americans, are far better off materially than even the richest people throughout most of history. A lot of poor people have air conditioning in the summer, heat in the winter, food, shelter, clothing, access to medical care, schools, libraries, transportation. They have tv's, computers, and cell phones. All that. The material wealth and comforts enjoyed by our poor would've been envied by the rich just a hundred years ago. Material poverty isn't their problem. At least not their biggest problem"

"So what do you think is, then?" Willis probed.

"The real poverty of our poor, and not just the poor, Willis, is spiritual. Spiritual impoverishment leads to chaos in many of their lives, and a lot of the people we work with are teetering on the brink of despair because of that chaos. They feel like they're dangling over a chasm clinging to a thread. Spiritual poverty takes away their pride and dignity and often makes their lives tawdry and squalid. We try to give them hope by showing them a better way to live, by giving them the spiritual resources to get them to a better place and a better life. We're trying to change their lives by changing their hearts."

"One way this spiritual poverty affects people," Loren interjected, "is the deterioration of the family. Fatherlessness among the poor lies at the root of almost every other problem plaguing their communities."

Caleb stopped walking and turned toward his brother to emphasize what he was about to say next. "It's the church's job to clean up the messes. The modern drift away from Christianity has been like a sudden ice storm on a crowded highway. Casualties are scattered everywhere. There's not much we can do about the ice, but we can give aid to the injured." The three men continued on toward the church building. "We're sort of EMTs in a way," Caleb added with a grin as he held open the church door for the others.

"It's one way of preaching the gospel," Loren added. St. Francis is supposed to have said that we should preach the gospel all the time and sometimes we should even use words. This is our way of doing that when we're not using words. In everything we do here we remind people that it comes from God, not from us. We're just his hands."

"How do you pay for all this?" Willis asked.

"Donors, businesspersons...there are lots of people in the city willing to help out financially as long as they know their money's being put to good use and not being wasted."

"Maybe there's a lesson in that for government," Caleb laughed.

"Our finance committee runs a small microfinance operation for people who need a loan for bills, or to keep a small business afloat, whatever it may be," Loren explained. "Members and friends of the congregation contribute to the loan and get paid back over time. They can recycle their loan to another borrower or take their repayment in cash. Borrowers benefit by getting zero-interest loans that enable them to stay solvent or build their businesses. It doesn't always work, but for the most part these loans have been indispensible for a lot of our people."

Once inside the building Loren said there was one more stop he wanted to make. "We offer assistance to parents who need help in managing money, being a good spouse, or parenting skills. That's what this meeting is." He pointed toward a room just ahead of them in the hallway. Inside seven women were sitting in a circle having a lively discussion. They grew quiet when they saw Loren and his companions enter.

"*Buenos días*, ladies."

"*Buenos*, Pastor Loren." When the women saw Caleb their eyes widened with excitement and emotion. They collectively showered him with exclamations of delight that his *niña* was safely home. Caleb was deeply touched by their outpouring of love and concern.

"Sounds like you're having a good discussion," Loren observed once calm was restored. The women nodded that indeed they were.

"What's the topic for today?"

A giggle rippled around the group. "We're discussing, 'What men want in a woman'," a stout woman named Alita answered with a sly grin.

"Ah. A delicate question. Maybe you should have some men here to give you their opinion," Loren suggested drolly.

"No, they wouldn't be any help," Alita retorted. "Men don't know what they really want." The women all laughed.

"Or they want the wrong thing," offered another woman, and the group laughed again.

"So what answers have you come up with?" Loren inquired.

"Well, we think men want to be admired and respected. They want their woman to look up to him as though he were the most important man in the world," another participant named Clarisse replied.

"And what do women want from a man?" Loren asked.

"Pretty much the same thing, I guess," Clarisse continued. "To treat them with respect, to be faithful, to be a good provider and good father to their children."

"Too many men don't respect their women." Alita tacked the thought on as an addendum.

"And why do you suppose that is?"

The women were silent, as though they were reluctant to answer, until Clarisse spoke up. "It's because too many women think they can get the man to respect and love her if she gives him her body with no strings attached. Usually it doesn't work." Clarisse looked at the other women in the group as if enlisting their assent.

"A lot of men are like children," she continued as her friends nodded. "When a mother gives her child everything he wants and doesn't demand anything in return the child grows up without respecting the mother. When a woman gives a man everything he wants without demanding commitment she loses his respect. At least that's what I think."

A murmur of general agreement rose from the group.

"Sounds like there's a lot of wisdom in this room," Loren observed with approval.

The women laughed again. "Sad to say, Pastor, whatever wisdom we have we got the hard way," one of the women declared.

"Unfortunately, that's how most people do it," Loren replied. As he spoke he noticed that one of the women who usually attended this meeting was missing.

"Where's Margarita? Isn't she usually in your group?"

The women suddenly went quiet. Loren looked at them with a quizzical expression. Alita explained. "She's beaten up. It's Rico, her *macho* pig of a boyfriend. We told her she's got to get rid of him, but she won't listen. Now her face is a mess, and she doesn't want anyone to see her. She's still getting her wisdom the hard way."

Another member of the group, Rosa, offered a supplement to Alita's opinion of Margarita's boyfriend. "He's the kind of man who's kind and sweet and full of flattery at first. A woman falls in love with such a man because he's cute, too. Then, when he gets what he wants, he turns into an animal. They fight, he beats her, but she won't leave him because she's still in love with the kind, sweet flatterer that she thought he was, and she can't see that that's not who he really is at all."

Loren was upset by this news. "Did she call the police?"

"No, she won't press charges. She thinks it's her fault he treats her bad, or she thinks she can get him to change, I don't know which. She's had *dos hijos* to him, and he doesn't change. I don't know what's the matter with her."

Caleb put his hand lightly on Loren's arm to interrupt and spoke to Alita. The boyfriend's name had reminded him of something.

"Do you know what Margarita's boyfriend's last name is?" Caleb asked.

Alita didn't seem to know and glanced at some of the other women sitting in the circle. One of them contemptuously spat out the name: "*Gardonez.*"

Caleb looked at Loren who was at first only vaguely aware that there was something significant about the name. Then it came to him. He was visibly shaken as he addressed himself to the women, "Do any of you know where this Gardonez lives?"

The woman who had known the surname answered, "He lives wherever somebody will give him a bed. I think he's living with his uncle right now, but you should stay away from him, Pastor, he's a very bad man, that Rico. He's spawn of the devil. So is his uncle."

"Do you know the uncle's name or address?"

"No, but I can get it later today, I think, but please stay away from him, too, Pastor. People say he has killed men. He struts around with a gun in his belt as if daring someone to look at him wrong. Everybody in the neighborhood is afraid of him."

"Don't worry, I'm not going to interfere, but if you could text me that address this afternoon I'd be grateful. *Gracias*."

As they walked down the hall toward the church exit, Caleb was searching in his wallet for the card with Michael's cell number on it.

"What's that all about?" Willis asked.

"Enrico Gardonez is the name of the man that was implicated in Alicia's abduction," Caleb answered. "He may also have had something to do with the disappearance of Michael's daughter. At least Michael seems to think so."

"I think we need to give this information to the police, Caleb," Loren advised.

"Yeah, but I promised Michael I'd let him know if I heard something. I at least want to tell him what we found out."

Just as they reached the door Alita came hurrying down the hall holding a slip of paper.

"One of the ladies remembered where Rico's uncle lives. His name is Roberto. She didn't know the street number, but she wrote the directions down on this."

She handed the paper to Loren, who passed it to Caleb. "*Gracias*, Alita. Thank the lady for us."

CHAPTER TEN

Willis left his brother and Loren at Loren's office and drove across town to his one o'clock class at the college. His mind was whirling. What he'd seen at Holt's church had somehow rekindled in him something that had long lain dormant. Sitting behind the wheel of his car he was aware of a nostalgia for some vague, indefinable experience from his adolescence, something he'd lost or outgrown. Perhaps it was the sense of purpose, of doing something deeply meaningful like his brother and the others at Holt's church were doing. One reason he had found it fairly easy to leave the church and renounce his faith was that the church he'd grown up in did little to provide young people with a sense of purpose. That, coupled with the inability of the adults in the church to provide answers to tough questions, just made it all seem like so much play-acting, and when he went off to college it became irrelevant to his life.

Ever since his decision to abandon the religion of his youth and immerse himself in literature as a kind of substitute Willis had adopted, quite without being conscious of it, the mindset that's not so much hostile to Christianity as it is simply indifferent to it. He never felt the need for God, he thought to himself. He never felt like there was anything missing. Yet now he was starting to see that all these years something had been pestering him like an insistent child gently tugging at his sleeve. A yearning that he'd managed to repress before it even rose to the level of a conscious thought was now elbowing its way to the forefront of his mind.

He resisted, but it pushed back. He imagined himself fighting something undefined and indiscernible. His will seemed locked in combat with an invisible antagonist. The struggle reminded him of a scene in a movie he'd seen once in which a schizophrenic character in the film found himself in a street fight with a foe that was a complete illusion, except Willis was no longer certain that his opponent, whatever it was, was an illusion.

Entering the classroom building he made his way to the faculty lounge for another cup of coffee before class. Several colleagues who'd been sitting about the room all jumped to their feet with broad smiles when he walked in. They'd heard the good news about Alicia and were eager to tell him how happy they were that his niece had been rescued.

Willis thanked them all, poured himself a cup of coffee, sat down at a table and disclosed to them what he knew of her rescue, which wasn't much. Nevertheless, the tale held his fellow professors spell-bound.

Toward the end of his account he mentioned the support Caleb had gotten from his church and, for reasons he couldn't have explained, even to himself, he went into some detail about his discussion Friday night with Caleb's pastor.

As he recounted the discussion, highlighting some of the give and take between Holt and himself, he noticed that one of his colleagues, a bearded, slovenly philosophy professor, maintained an expression of obvious disdain on his face. Willis paused his narrative and looked at him as if to ask what it was that was bothering him. The philosopher–his name was Chadsworth Watkins–simply lowered his eyes and shook his head. Willis was curious as to what he'd said that caused Watkins to react this way. Neither man said anything until Watkins finally concluded that Willis wasn't going to move on without an explanation.

He lifted his hands in a gesture of resignation and admitted that he was surprised that Willis, whom he knew to be a man of reason and eminent good sense, was consorting with religious people who, in his opinion, were the bane of American society.

His words stunned Willis. Why was the company he chose to keep, Willis asked Watkins, a subject that should concern *him*? The philosophy professor just waved it off as if he wanted to forget the matter, but Willis, his visit that morning to Holt's church still fresh in his mind, insisted that these were good people and that Watkins was being most unfair and prejudicial in his judgment of them.

Watkins possessed neither a sense of humor nor a sense of irony and, like most who are bereft of that particular combination of traits, was incapable of self-deprecation. He also enjoyed a reputation as a fiery, militant advocate of far-left politics and radical secularism. He was outspoken in his views, disparaging and insulting to those who disagreed with him, and it was well-known that, like many who shared his political leanings, he despised Christianity and Christians. He thought from things Willis had said in the past that he was a sympathetic ally and was taken aback by Willis' reaction in the present circumstance.

The three other professors in the lounge grew quiet. This confrontation was an awkward, embarrassing development which made all of them uneasy, but what happened next made them even more uncomfortable. Watkins had been offended by Willis' reproach, and was not a man to turn the other cheek nor suffer offense graciously.

"You may think they're good people, Hoffmeyer, but in fact they're a bunch of simple-minded bigots. They're haters. They hate women, they hate gays, they hate science, they hate anyone different from themselves. They're blessedly ignorant of the fact that their world of spirits and miracles has been made obsolete by science for the last two hundred years. They're in fact living in a world of self-delusion."

Willis sensed anger beginning to smolder in his breast, but he said nothing. Watkins was impugning people whom he dearly loved–his parents, his brother and sister-in-law–and whether he agreed with Watkins' characterization of Christians in general he profoundly resented the implication that his family was a bunch of hateful ignoramuses.

One of the faculty members in the room sought to relieve the tension by venturing a question of Professor Watkins. "But Chad, don't you think that the loss of religious mystery has left us in some ways impoverished and empty?"

"Only in the sense that if all children's fairy tales disappeared we'd be impoverished," Watkins snorted, "but children's fairy tales aren't pernicious, 'Christianism' is. They ought to all be required to enlist in a deprogramming facility."

The room was so quiet the heartbeats were almost audible.

Watkins dimly perceived that he'd crossed the line of propriety. "Look, I'm sorry, but that's just how I feel," he added by way of explaining his outburst. "These people are idiots. Skepticism is the litmus test of a person's intelligence, credulousness is the mark of a fool."

Willis was now furious. The slow burn was about to burst into an inferno. Waves of anger spread through his body, building pressure like steam in a closed pot. This man was libeling not just his family, but the good people he'd met Friday night and earlier that day as well. It was all Willis could do to control himself.

"Just throw them into concentration camps, should we?" Willis' voice was ice cold, but his face was florid, and the steam was pushing hard against the lid of the pot. "Why not shoot them, too, Watkins?"

"Oh, I wouldn't go that far," was Watkins' sarcastic riposte. His tone did nothing to dampen Willis' indignation.

"Maybe not, but you're clearing the ground for those who would. There are people all around the world today, mostly Christians, living in fear for their lives, being beheaded and buried alive by people who think just like you do. For heaven's sake, you sound like a Nazi, Watkins."

"Look, Hoffmeyer, of course I exaggerated, but these people you seem to suddenly be so fond of are intolerant morons. You know that. I've heard you come close to saying as much yourself."

"So your solution is to not tolerate them?" Willis was having difficulty controlling his voice. His anger was gripping the volume knob, demanding permission to turn it all the way up, but Willis didn't want to create any more of a scene than he already had.

"Precisely," Watkins replied, missing the irony, "Just as we wouldn't tolerate a virus if we could eliminate it. I'm not saying that we should eliminate *them*, but their ideas are dangerous, and they need to be counteracted. Their ideas need to be expunged from society if we're going to continue to make social and scientific progress."

Willis rose from his chair, locked his eyes directly on Watkins, and slowly, stonily, said to him, "You don't have any idea what you're talking about. Whatever I think about their beliefs, they're good people, and they're doing a lot more to make this world better than you are." Turning his back, he strode out of the room.

A smirk spread across Watkins' face. "What's his problem? Did they baptize him or something over the weekend?" Watkins punctuated the question with an abrupt snigger, but no one else saw the humor. They all got up and quietly left, leaving him sitting at the table by himself.

When Caleb called Michael to inform him of Enrico Gardonez's whereabouts he added that he'd also be passing the information on to the Baltimore City Police Department and the FBI agents working Alicia's case.

Michael thanked him for the tip and immediately called Carlos and Danny to tell them he was headed to the location Caleb Hoffmeyer had provided him. He asked them to grab a cab and join him as soon as they could.

The residence was actually an apartment on the second floor of a boarded-up grocery store in the midst of a depressingly dreary neighborhood. At least this was a fair description of the block in which the old grocery store sat. The quadrant consisted of several vacant lots strewn with weeds, rubbish, broken glass, and old tires with a few scattered, poorly maintained houses interspersed here and there. The businesses, such as they were, consisted of a liquor store and a check cashing establishment that operated out of a small, grubby shack.

The desolate landscape was rendered even more dismal by a low, grey autumn sky from which a light drizzle had been falling all afternoon. Fallen leaves, newspapers and other trash scudded and swirled along the street, propelled by gusts of chilly wind.

Neither of the businesses appeared to be attracting clientele at the moment, and only a few people, mostly children, could be seen around any of the row homes further down the street. Graffiti was sprayed on almost every wall. A couple of blocks away stood apartment buildings, basketball courts, and shops, but the block Michael surveyed from his parked car seemed as bleak and forlorn as a lunar landscape.

Michael studied the building in which he understood Enrico Gardonez might be residing. It sat on a corner lot bounded by a street in front and another on the right. To the left of the old store there was an alley that separated it from an abandoned brick house. An outside stairway attached to the structure led from the alley to a second floor landing and a door. From what Michael could see that was the only entrance into the apartment.

Michael decided to sit in his car and keep an eye on the place from an inconspicuous spot down the street. He was curious to see if the police would show up to roust Enrico and was half-hoping that they wouldn't since he wanted to question him himself. A half hour later movement in his rear view mirror drew his attention, and he saw Carlos and Danny approaching his car on foot in the light rain. At their request the cabbie had let them out a couple blocks to the east and they'd walked the rest of the way.

A few minutes after they climbed into Michael's car a half dozen police cruisers pulled up in front of the old store and a platoon of officers, acting on Caleb's tip and accompanied by what may have been

FBI agents, emerged. They milled around a bit talking on their radios before several of them ascended the stairs. The CSR team watched three police officers knock on the door and enter the apartment with weapons drawn. Fifteen minutes later they reemerged with someone, presumably Enrico, in handcuffs. They loaded him into one of the squad cars and left. Other officers carried out a box containing what were probably the suspected felon's personal items, including his weapons and computer.

"Huh. Well, that's that. Maybe the cops'll get some information out of him," Danny speculated somewhat hopefully. "Who knows what they'll find on his computer."

"I'm sure it's downloads of the Great Books of Western Civilization," Michael replied dryly without shifting his gaze from the activity in front of the store.

The team clung to the tenuous hope that Laryssa might still be in Baltimore. In fact that was why Danny had asked Luis if he'd had any African-American girls come his way in the last couple of years. Luis' negative answer afforded them a slim basis for thinking she might still be in the city, but of course, she could be anywhere in the world, or just as likely, though no one would say it, dead. Right now, though, Michael was clinging to the hope that Enrico knew something about any missing girls in Baltimore and that the police interrogators would eventually get it out of him.

They hung around for a while after the police left and were just getting ready to head back to the hotel themselves when two cars pulled up in front of the abandoned grocery. Five men stepped out of the vehicles and climbed the stairs to the second floor landing. The door opened, and a sixth man appeared in the doorway. The team concluded that the man in the doorway was Uncle Roberto whom the CSR guys began calling "Uncle Bob." It was anyone's guess who the other men were, but they didn't appear to be there to discuss the Great Books.

It was beginning to grow dark. The few people who'd been visible on the street seemed now to disappear into the relative security of their homes. Michael and his companions decided to stick around. They were a little curious as to why these men would show up shortly after Enrico had been taken into custody. Maybe the one thing had nothing to do with the other, but they didn't have anything else to do so they decided to wait awhile and see what might develop.

Danny volunteered to walk a couple of blocks to a MacDonald's they'd passed earlier to buy them all some dinner.

Carlos reclined his seat, leaned back and closed his eyes. He knew Michael would keep watch on the apartment for both of them. He reflected on the pain and guilt Michael lived with everyday because of the loss of his daughter. He'd grown fond of Michael over the two years they'd worked together and felt deeply sorry for him. Thinking of Michael's loss led him to remembrances of his niece, the young woman raped and left for dead with her parents in Big Bend National Park, and that horrifying reminiscence led in turn to think of his own parents' anguish in the wake of that awful crime. His thoughts then jumped to recollections of a long series of extractions in which he'd participated, culminating in the most recent operation to rescue Alicia Hoffmeyer.

In the course of these missions he encountered so many bestial, cruel men that it was easy to think that such animals dominated the human race. So much evil, how does one fight against it? That thought brought to mind the conversation he'd had with Reverend Holt two days earlier on that very theme. Was Holt right when he claimed that evil is only evil if it's a violation of the law of God and that in the absence of God evil is just a word we give to things which the people who decide such matters find distasteful?

Carlos didn't like that idea very much, but something about it nevertheless rang true. He recalled many of the men he had known and admired for their goodness. So many of them, especially the ones he knew as he was growing up, were priests and monks, and the recollection of these good and gentle men churned up a wistful yearning in his soul, a desire for something he couldn't quite name, something which seemed to elude him, like a mirage eludes the one who tries to approach it. Talking with a pastor in a church touched his heart, made him feel somehow closer to heaven, even though it wasn't a Catholic church and Holt wasn't a Catholic priest. He wondered if what he'd felt wasn't maybe the breath of a relentless Hound on his neck.

He decided for the first time since he was in combat in the military to say a silent prayer. He prayed for all three of them, just in case the others neglected to do it for themselves.

A half hour later the neighborhood was so dark it was hard to see much. A few street lights, shrouded in the misty precipitation, shed a dull, yellowish glow on the pavement, and most of the houses and apartments had their lights turned off or their shades drawn.

Over the burgers and fries Danny brought back the team debated whether they should check out Uncle Bob's apartment. They ultimately agreed there wasn't much point. The police probably looked it over pretty thoroughly when they were there a couple of hours before. They decided to leave and depend on the police interrogation of Enrico to uncover anything that might help them bring closure to Laryssa's disappearance.

As Michael reached to turn the key in the ignition a light went on in a ground level window below the boarded-up grocery store. The window was under the stairway on the side of the building. That seemed odd. Why would anyone be down *there*? Did the police go down into that basement when they were there?

They figured they may as well take a peek.

Collars turned up against the chill and hands thrust into their pockets, the three men moved quietly down the street toward the abandoned store. Just as Danny was bending down to see what, if anything, he could discern going on inside the basement, the light went out. He peered in anyway. The window was dirty and partially covered with a curtain. He couldn't see much in the darkened room, but he nevertheless thought he could just barely make out dark silhouettes, like people sitting on a bed.

He walked back to where Michael and Carlos were standing in the shadows to give him cover should he need it and recounted what he thought he saw. It could be nothing. It could just be that that's where Uncle Bob keeps his crazy aunt, but it certainly seemed strange.

Carlos crept quietly up the wooden stairway, slick from the rain, and peered in the window at the landing. A curtain partially obscured his view, but he was able to see four men sitting around a table just getting a card game started. A fifth man was lounging on a lazy-boy watching television. He couldn't see the sixth man. Several of the men had removed their jackets and were clearly armed. He assumed they all were.

"It looks like a meeting of the Rotary Club," Carlos observed facetiously. "Do we want to break up a card game involving some of Baltimore's finest citizens and risk a shootout just to ask them if we can have a look around their apartment?"

"It'd seem rude," Danny opined, as they walked back to the car to discuss the situation.

Despite their pretense of insouciance they were in fact growing increasingly concerned that they were wandering well beyond CSR's mission. Danny and Carlos worried that they were exposing themselves to running afoul of the police or, worse, risking life and limb in a gun fight with a bunch of hoodlums for no clear reason, a risk Carlos likened to those he was asked to take in the military.

Michael assured them that he'd understand if they wanted to leave, but he was going to stick around for a while. This was the first thread he'd come upon in his search for his daughter, and he was going to follow it as long as there was any chance it might lead to something.

His friends were quiet. Rain, heavier now, splattered on the windshield and tapped a rhythm on the roof. Despite their misgivings they knew they weren't going to leave Michael alone, and they knew, too, that if they were in his place they'd do the same thing he was doing.

"Hand me some of those fries," Carlos said to Danny sitting in the back seat. The fries were cold, but Danny grabbed a few for himself and passed the bag to Carlos. Changing the subject was their unspoken way of telling Michael that they weren't going to leave him.

Michael, however, still wasn't sure what his companions were going to do. He looked over at Carlos sitting beside him munching a mouthful of cold french fries. Carlos said nothing but simply raised his eyebrows and held out the bag to Michael as if to offer him some. Michael smiled and held up his hand in a gesture of polite refusal. He knew then that Carlos and Danny were with him.

The three men turned to wondering if there was a way they could get into the basement from the outside, but as they were in the midst of puzzling over this logistical problem the basement light blinked on again. Shortly, two men appeared from behind the building with a girl. Where'd *she* come from? It was much too dark to tell at this distance anything more about her than that she was a young woman.

The men stuffed her in their car, rather unchivalrously, the CSR team judged. All three of them realized at the same instant that this girl had been in the basement below the old store, but if so, why were the lights kept off? Apparently the police had no reason to go down there when they came for Enrico. It probably never occurred to them to do so.

The men who brought her out were evidently taking her some-where she was reluctant to go. "Maybe we should check this out," Michael said softly. As he uttered those words one of the men walked back toward the basement. The other got into the backseat of the car next to the girl.

"Let's go," Carlos said, checking his weapon and grabbing a fistful of nylon flexi-cuffs from the glove compartment.

A few miles west of Cuidad Juarez two Mexican police cars and a van made their way along a dusty road to a solitary house outside a small village. Luis was handcuffed in the back seat of one of the cars.

He was unable to tell the police where he'd been kept by the *gringos* who had kidnapped him, killed his friends, and stolen a great deal of his money, but he divulged to them everything he could, including a grisly recitation of the horrible fate of one of his clients, a man named Carlos. He did not, however, admit to any of the scurrilous allegations made against him in the information the CSR team had affixed to him when they left him at the police station.

A resident of the village had reported seeing a group of *americanos* driving up this same lane to an abandoned house, now locked up, which sat at the end of the road. This was a tip the authorities decided should be investigated. The van was a mobile forensics lab which, based on Luis' testimony and the expectation of finding copious quantities of blood splattered everywhere, they assumed they might need. Once the vehicles pulled up in front of the house two police officers disembarked and walked around to the back to look for the dismembered corpse that Luis assured them they'd find there.

Meanwhile, other officers forced open the front door, and Luis led them downstairs to the basement. Standing precisely where Carlos had been bound to the pole *El Jefe* looked around uncomprehendingly. The steel column was there, but the room was spotless. It must have been cleaned up, he thought, but other than when they hosed it

down, he didn't know when they could have scrubbed it so clean unless somebody came in to tidy it up after he'd been taken away.

The forensics technicians said that if the sort of butchery Luis described had in fact taken place here they'd find traces of blood that might be overlooked by the naked eye. They turned off the lights and sprayed a luminol solution around the room. The iron atoms in the blood protein hemoglobin bind with a chemical in the luminol causing it to give off a bluish glow. It only lasts for about thirty seconds, but that would be long enough to enable them to detect any blood that had spattered on the floor, walls, or ceiling. Yet, when they sprayed the solution there was no glow anywhere.

Luis was incredulous. "There must be," he insisted in Spanish. "Try the other side of the wall. That's where I was when I saw the blood washing down the drain."

They sprayed around the drain and observed a faint hint of blue. This partly vindicated Luis, but surely there had to be blood everywhere from such carnage as the *gringos* inflicted. Why wasn't it there?

"That might be blood," the tech said in Spanish pointing to a residue around the drain, "but it doesn't look right. There are other things, like bleach, which can give a false positive. I'll scrape up a sample and test it in the van."

Ten minutes later the police and a mystified Luis emerged from the house. He knew he'd seen blood flow under the wall and down the drain near where he'd been sitting. Surely they couldn't have cleaned the place so thoroughly that nothing of that man's gore remained in the basement. Moreover, the officers who'd searched the area outside the house had found nothing. This perplexed Luis even more.

As they walked toward the police cruisers the technician in the van called the officers over.

"It's not blood. I think the glow was caused by a compound called iron nitrate. I'll have to run more tests back at the lab, but I'm pretty sure I know what this man saw." He held up his i-pad which was showing a picture of something that looked like a quart of motor oil.

He looked at Luis and pointed to the image on the screen, "*Sangre falsa*," he stated matter-of-factly, glancing at Luis who was staring at the picture on the i-pad in stupefied disbelief. Fake blood. "You can buy it *por cuatro pesos* at Walmart," he added as if to amplify Luis' embarrassment.

Luis stared for a few more seconds at the screen and then, despite his humiliation, began to chuckle quietly to himself. Shaking his head and laughing in a mix of anger and admiration of the cleverness of the *gringos* and how he'd been "played" by them, he sauntered over to the cruiser for the long ride back to the prison in Cuidad Juarez.

❦

The three men from CSR quietly and swiftly approached the car from behind. Danny quickly flung open the door and pointed his weapon at the startled man's face. Carlos on the other side opened the door and gently helped the girl from the car. Michael covered the house lest any of its denizens wandered out.

Danny ordered the man out of the car, threatened to shoot him if he uttered a word unbidden, frisked him, disarmed him, took his phone, cuffed him with flexi-cuffs, and gagged him with the greasy bandana he'd been wearing on his head.

Michael looked carefully at the girl but didn't recognize her. The rain had eased and was falling now as a light mist.

"Don't be afraid," he said soothingly. "We're not going to hurt you. Are you with this man because you want to be or because you don't have a choice?"

The girl was too frightened to respond, and she was shivering in the chill, wet air. Michael changed the question.

"Are there any other girls inside?"

She nodded.

"How many?"

"One."

In the basement?"

"Yes."

"Is there a door to the basement around back?"

She nodded again and started to cry. "These men kept me here like a prisoner for months," she finally managed to blurt out, "the other girl longer."

"Where are you from?"

"D.C."

"Do you want to go home?"

She nodded yes with tears streaming down her face.

"This man," he motioned toward Carlos who was holding her arm for support, "is going to take you to a car down the street. He's going to put you in the back seat, and I want you to lock the door and lay down on the seat so no one sees you. We'll be back as soon as we can. What's your name?"

"Dominique."

"Okay, you're safe now, Dominique."

"Bring him with us," he said to Danny as he motioned toward the prisoner.

Michael, Danny and their bound and gagged hostage made their way cautiously toward the back of the building. It was dark, but a sliver of dim light shone through the basement door which had been left slightly ajar. A man could be heard yelling angrily in Spanish at someone inside.

Five cement steps descended from street level to the basement doorway. Michael went first.

CHAPTER ELEVEN

Willis shook his head slightly as he passed a bowl of salad across the table to Marie. The two were recapitulating the events of their respective workdays over dinner, and Willis was still nettled by his encounter that afternoon with the odious Chadsworth Watkins in the faculty lounge.

"Why would anyone say something like that even if they were thinking it?" He asked Marie as he finished reprising his exchange with Watkins.

"Well, maybe he's had some bad experiences with religious people, Willis. Heaven knows enough other people have. Anyway, he sounds like he's bitter about something."

"A man can be bitter without being cruel."

"Maybe *he* can't."

Marie had more than a passing familiarity with bitterness herself. Until she met Willis most of the key men in her world had, in one way or another, made her life miserable. Her father deserted her mother, her, and her siblings when she was eleven. Her mother then proceeded to run through a series of repugnant boyfriends until she finally married again when Marie was fourteen, but this new stepfather was unable to keep his hands off Marie. She simultaneously loathed him and lived in fear of his advances.

Once she left for college she never returned home, but desperate for stability and security in her life, she wound up in her senior year undertaking a precipitous marriage to a man who gambled heavily, drank even more heavily, and proved incapable of grasping the simple principle that upon marriage a man is expected to forsake all others. Determined not to end up like her mother, Marie divorced the cad after a brief and unpleasant union. People who knew her were astonished that she rolled the dice again with Willis, but she did, and it had worked out well.

Even so, she was a woman who carried a lot of scars and a lot of bitterness. Caleb and Patty were quite sure that this was the major reason for her antipathy toward Christianity which she saw as oppressively patriarchal and devoted to a loving heavenly father to whom she simply could not relate.

"I've heard of people," Willis said as he piled some spaghetti on his plate, "who abandoned Christianity because of bad experiences with other Christians. I wonder how many atheists become Christians because of bad experiences with other atheists. People like Watkins."

Marie decided to remain silent and let her husband vent. He clearly needed to unburden himself of the negative emotion he'd accumulated that day, but despite the anger he had felt that afternoon, he shared his assessment of Watkins with Marie in a calm, faintly amused, tone.

"Watkins is the kind of guy who thinks that only what he has to say is interesting and worth listening to. He assumes that the proper order of things is for him to speak, mostly about himself, and for everyone else to listen. The guy has an ego completely out of proportion to any justification for it."

"You shouldn't let him upset you."

"Yeah, I know, but I'd just come from Caleb's church. He and Holt showed me what they do there, and I have to say I was affected by it. I didn't tell Caleb that," Willis added with a slight smirk, "but it really is remarkable what they do, Marie. I think

I misjudged Holt. I had a stereotype of what he'd be, and he doesn't fit it at all. Maybe I'm as bad as Watkins."

Willis uttered this last sentence almost under his breath. He didn't really believe it, and a moment later he was ripping into his antagonist again.

"Anyway, for Watkins to essentially call Caleb and Patty–and mom, for that matter–ignorant bigots and to suggest they should be put in some prison because they're motivated by beliefs that've been motivating people for thousands of years to do the things Caleb's church is doing, isn't just cruel, it's stupid. It doesn't matter if their beliefs are all wrong. What matters is what kind of people they are."

He wasn't done. "If anyone's a bigot it's Watkins. He thinks that religious people are weak because in his mind they spend all their time thinking about the hereafter and don't do anything to improve the world they live in now. It's nonsense, but a man consumed by as much hatred as he is doesn't care whether his prejudices are true or not. All he cares about is whether they're useful in reinforcing his own self-image as being smarter than everybody else."

Willis sprinkled some Parmesan cheese on his spaghetti. "Caleb's church is trying to make life better for people living in awful circumstances, while people like Watkins sit in their air-conditioned offices, never having made anything better for anybody, and condemn those who do because they're motivated by a belief Watkins thinks is nuts. I don't know whether he's just stupid or if he's morally blind."

"Maybe you should take Professor Watkins to Caleb's church and show him around," Marie suggested with an impish grin.

"Yeah. Good luck with that," Willis said with a chuckle as he raised a forkful of pasta to his mouth. He lowered it without eating and laughed again. "You know, Marie, I think this is probably the first time in over twenty years I've defended people who were criticized for being Christian."

"Well," his wife replied in a faintly disdainful voice, "not many of them deserve to be defended."

Michael noiselessly descended the steps and squinted through the thin slit between the slightly opened door and the jamb. He could see no one, but he could hear a very angry man yelling at someone, then the sound of sobbing. Michael slowly and noiselessly pushed the door open. A thickly built man with long, scruffy hair wearing shorts and a white, perspiration-stained tank-top stood looming over a girl sitting on a bed with her knees drawn up and her face covered by her arms. His back was to Michael. The girl was wearing nothing but a flimsy nightgown and was in obvious emotional distress. The man, still yelling in Spanish, swung the back of his hand hard across the side of her head knocking her onto her back and sprawling her across the bed.

Michael's heart was pounding. He didn't know for sure whether he was intruding on a domestic quarrel or something even worse, and he reproached himself for not having questioned more thoroughly the handcuffed man standing with Danny at the top of the steps behind him about what exactly was going on in this house.

He quickly scanned the room. The bed across which the now hysterical girl was lying was arranged perpendicularly to the wall to his left. There was a small table with some dinner plates and magazines and a large, shabby arm chair against the wall to his right. A few items of clothing hung on hooks on the far wall. A toilet and shower were partitioned off in the far left corner of the room. The far wall divided the basement in half, and a doorway gave access to the other half. Michael assumed that there was a stairway on the other side of the wall leading to the upper floors of the building.

The man was grabbing at the girl's ankles in an attempt to pull her off the bed, all the while demanding in Spanish that she get up and go with him to the car.

Michael decided that he couldn't just stand there and watch this, nor could he turn around and leave. He had to make a move. Dominique had said that she and this girl had been held as prisoners, so Michael assumed that this was not likely a domestic dispute. Entering the basement he clutched his weapon in the pocket of his overcoat and, despite his nervousness, spoke softly and calmly.

"I think you should stop hitting the girl, *hombre*."

The man spun around, startled by the unfamiliar voice. A semi-automatic pistol was stuck in his belt.

"Who are you?" The question was salted with an obscenity.

Michael saw the gun in the man's pants, but pretended to ignore it. "It's not important who I am." He moved forward a couple of steps to get a better look at the girl's face, but she was holding her head in her hands, and he couldn't see her well. "I assume you are Roberto."

Roberto was bewildered. Who was this tall black man who appears out of nowhere and knows his name? He ruled out a return visit by the police. Nothing about Michael's approach indicated police. He assumed that the hand in his pocket gripped a gun else he wouldn't have been so bold, especially since Roberto knew this intruder could clearly see that he himself was armed.

Meanwhile, Danny had quietly prodded his prisoner down the steps and stood behind him in the darkness just beyond the doorway. Roberto, preoccupied with Michael, didn't notice.

At that moment the girl looked up at Michael. She stared for a couple of seconds, her eyes widening in shock and disbelief as recognition swept over her. Her mouth formed an inchoate word, but no sound came out. She seemed almost afraid that if she uttered the word aloud the man would dissolve like an apparition.

Michael's attention was riveted on Roberto. He still didn't realize who the girl on the bed was. Then her movement caught his eye and he recognized her immediately. A host of emotions surged through him all at once. After all this time. After two years of despair, of disappointed hopes, of yearning, of guilt. Here was his little girl in a cold, damp, moldy basement on a filthy bed, abused, molested, and beaten by the arrogant thug standing in front of him. But she was alive. He hoped to God he wasn't hallucinating.

Laryssa slid off the bed and walked slowly toward Michael, tears welling in her eyes, her chin quivering. Almost in slow motion, fearing that it was all too good to be true after two years of imprisonment, fear and abuse, she wrapped her arms around him, hugged him, and began to sob uncontrollably. "Daddy," she cried. "It's really you."

Michael put his arm around her, holding her tightly to himself. He wanted to hug her, to shower her with kisses, to tell her how much he loved her, but he couldn't allow his emotions to distract him from the threat posed by the smirking Roberto. His dark eyes glaring balefully at his daughter's rapist, Michael icily informed him, "She's mine. You're finished."

Roberto shrugged with an air of feigned resignation and indifference.

Michael's mind replayed the scene he took in as he first entered that squalid cellar–Roberto standing over his helpless daughter, viciously beating her as she tried feebly to fend off the blows. Welts and bruises covering her face. His anger was stoked to an incandescent rage which he could scarcely contain. His eyes locked menacingly on Roberto as he slowly guided Laryssa behind him with his left hand while gripping a .357 magnum in his pocket with his right. He anticipated that Roberto would make a play for the semi-automatic in his belt, but he'd already decided he was going to kill Roberto whether he went for his gun or not.

Suddenly, one of Roberto's friends appeared in the doorway across the room. Michael quickly drew his weapon from his coat pocket, and Roberto seized the opportunity presented by the distraction to grab for his own gun.

Michael raised his revolver on the threat in the doorway as Roberto snatched his firearm from his belt and brought it up in an arc toward Michael's chest. It was all unfolding in milliseconds, but Roberto never had the chance to fire. Unbeknownst to Laryssa's captor, Danny Howe had been keeping the laser sight of his own Glock .40 trained on the man's heavily tattooed torso throughout the entire confrontation. Two shots rang out in quick succession before Roberto could pull the trigger on Michael. Uncle Bob had kidnapped, tortured and raped his last victim.

Danny had neglected, however, to screw his silencer onto his gun. The sound of the shots reverberated in the basement like small explosions. The man in the opposite doorway ducked behind the wall for cover and called to the men upstairs who had heard the gunfire and were already racing toward the basement.

Danny calculated that there were now four men left of the six they'd originally counted in the apartment.

Michael hurried to wrap Laryssa in a blanket and get her out of the room while Danny, still standing in the doorway behind his hostage, covered the door across the room. The screen door slammed on the landing at the top of the outside stairway on the side of the house. At least one of the four was coming down those stairs and would soon be turning the corner to the back of the building. Danny swiveled to aim his handgun at the corner of the wall in anticipation.

Now there were footsteps from several men hurrying down the inside staircase. Michael pushed Laryssa to the floor behind the armchair against the wall to his right and crouched between the chair and his daughter with his gun pointed at the open doorway. A head appeared quickly in the doorway surveying the room and immediately disappeared back behind the wall. That cursory assessment was followed by the appearance of an automatic pistol, it looked like a 9mm micro UZI, spraying gunfire blindly into the room. The man was shooting without exposing himself to return fire.

Danny's prisoner struggled to be free of his grip. The prisoner knew he was in an exposed position standing almost directly across the room from where the UZI was showering everything with bullets, but his gag prevented him from yelling to his *compadre* not to shoot. The machine pistol appeared again and another burst of gunfire perforated the walls and furniture.

Carlos had secured Dominique in the car, instructing her to lie down in the back and keep the doors locked. He had just started back up the street when he heard the pop of gunfire. He increased his pace to a sprint, racing up the street toward the old grocery store and arriving just as the man who had come out by way of the door at the top of the stairs was scampering down the steps. When the man reached the bottom he ran straight into Carlos who appeared out of the shadows and the muzzle of whose gun was less than six inches from the man's nose. Carlos disarmed him and used a flexi-cuff to strap him to the end post of the wrought iron railing. He then bounded up the stairs and into the second floor apartment searching for the door that led to the inside stairway that would take him down to the basement.

Michael assumed that the wall behind which the man with the UZI was sheltered was mere drywall and plaster nailed to a few 2 x 4 studs–not enough to stop a volley from his .357 magnum. A second later the man stuck the automatic pistol out again and fired another blind burst into the room. Michael aimed several rounds into the wall about eight inches to the right of the door frame. Screams of pain signaled that at least one of the rounds had struck home.

Michael knew, however, that the longer they stayed in that basement the less tenable their position became. These guys were probably on the phone calling for reinforcements, and if reinforcements didn't show up the police certainly would, and soon. Michael wasn't sure which would be worse. They couldn't stay where they were much longer.

He peered over the armrest of the chair to assess the situation, wondering where Carlos was. All he could hear were the moans of the man he had wounded through the drywall. Laryssa was pressed against the wall behind him, terrified, her knees drawn up to her chin and her hands covering her head. As Michael raised up to look over the chair, a second assailant who had picked up the wounded man's automatic pistol jumped into the doorway and fired a half dozen rounds directly into the chair.

Michael shifted in front of Laryssa to protect her with his body. As he did so several of the bullets ripped through the upholstery, one striking him above the clavicle, and another ripping into his torso, shattering a rib. The force of the impact knocked him back into his daughter.

Danny didn't know that Carlos had neutralized the threat posed by the man coming down the outside stairs, and he was trying to keep an eye on the corner of the building behind him while also watching the doorway across the room. When he heard the shots that struck Michael he pivoted to return fire, but the man retreated from the doorway and back behind the wall before he could be hit. Danny was about to fire into the wall, as Michael had done, in hopes of hitting his target, but just as he took aim he could hear Carlos at the top of the stairs yelling at the men at the bottom to freeze. Danny hesitated, but the momentary pause allowed the man who had just wounded Michael to wheel and send a burst of fire toward Carlos who quickly stepped back behind the door frame. The man emptied the magazine of his gun at Carlos, but none of the shots came close to their intended target.

Danny responded by unleashing several rounds into the wall, but none of his bullets found their mark either. Carlos peered quickly around the corner and saw three men at the bottom of the steps, the one shot by Michael writhing on the floor, another ducking from Danny's fire while trying to reload the UZI automatic pistol, the third holding a revolver but not showing much inclination to do anything with it. Carlos fired three rounds in quick succession at the man with the UZI, but only the first was necessary. The other man at the bottom of the steps quickly dropped his revolver and surrendered, begging not to be shot.

Danny fastened his prisoner to a drain pipe while Carlos secured the man who had surrendered to the banister at the bottom of the stairs.

Danny was the first to get to Michael and quickly tried to stanch the flow of blood into his chest cavity while Carlos called 911. Michael was having trouble breathing, and Laryssa was trembling with fear from the violence and from seeing her father so badly hurt.

"Hang on buddy, help'll be here soon," Danny encouraged as he glanced at Laryssa.

Michael's breaths were coming in gasps as he lay in his daughter's lap, his head cradled in her arms, her tears falling on his face as she tried gently to wipe them with her hand. The father she had rejected never stopped looking for her, never stopped trying to rescue her from the degradation in which she'd been imprisoned for almost two years. Now his life was draining out of his body. He'd given everything for her. She'd never forgive herself for the way she'd treated him, and she knew she could never thank him enough for the sacrifice he was making for her.

"Oh, daddy, please don't leave me. I'm so sorry, I'm so sorry. I love you daddy." She repeated the words, weeping almost hysterically and hugging his head tightly to her heart.

Sirens wailed out in the street. Danny ran to direct the EMTs to the basement. As they entered the room they saw Roberto lying motionless on the floor and stopped to check him.

"No, no," Carlos insisted impatiently, "This man, here," he demanded, motioning toward Michael. "This man needs help *now*."

The EMTs administered first aid, placed Michael on a gurney, and wheeled him to the MICU. Laryssa went with them. Other ambulances and police cruisers were arriving. The night was ablaze with flashing red and blue lights reflecting off the mist.

As the police rushed from the street to the back of the building they were startled to see first the man trussed to the outside stair railing on the side of the building and then another tied to a pipe at the back of the building. Inside they found yet a third man bound to the banister of the inside stairway. Nearby, one man still moaned in agony from gunshot wounds, and two men lay dead.

Carlos and Danny pretty much figured that their career with CSR, and maybe CSR itself, had come to an end. They laid their weapons on the bed and waited for the police to take them into custody.

Michael was rushed to the ER at Johns Hopkins Hospital only a few blocks from where he was shot. Laryssa was put in a wheel chair and taken to another part of the facility for examination. Doctors immediately set to work to get the wounded man stabilized and drain blood and other fluids from his lungs. His pulse was weak and failing.

Michael was dimly aware of medical personnel around him, their voices sounding distant and faint. Then everything faded into blackness and silence. He felt himself drifting as though separating from his body. The darkness broke and he perceived himself hovering above himself, watching the medical staff working feverishly on the version of himself that lay motionless on the table. He could see tubes in his mouth and another in his chest. Something had evidently gone wrong and the doctors were trying desperately to resuscitate him. He thought the scene odd because he wasn't down there.

Danny and Carlos were taken to precinct headquarters for questioning and booking. The arresting officers were extremely curious as to what exactly had happened at the abandoned grocery store, and why. They were even more curious about who these three men were who had bested members of one of Baltimore's most notorious and violent gangs. They were also keenly interested in questioning Laryssa and Dominique about how they came to be in that basement prison.

The police permitted the CSR guys a couple of calls. Carlos called John who, immediately upon hearing the news, left Washington for Baltimore. On his way out the door he hurriedly texted everyone associated with CSR, and as he pulled onto the I-495 beltway he called a lawyer who represented CSR whenever legal assistance was needed.

Danny searched through the contacts list in his cell phone for the number Loren Holt had given him when he and Carlos visited on Saturday. When Loren answered his phone Danny explained briefly what happened and where Michael was. He thought it would be good for a pastor to be at the hospital for Michael and Laryssa.

As soon as the call from Danny ended Loren and Olivia left for Johns Hopkins and contacted the Hoffmeyers while on the way to fill them in. The two couples arrived at the hospital at about the same time. Caleb and Patty brought Alicia. They'd scarcely let her out of their sight since she was returned to them the previous week. John arrived forty five minutes later.

Michael watched with a semi-detached curiosity as the staff below him ran through the procedures for reviving a patient who had flat-lined. Suddenly he found himself immersed in a brilliant, indescribable effulgence, a light so bright it was painful to look at. Notwithstanding its searing intensity, he felt drawn to it and thought to himself that if this is what it is to die it wasn't so bad.

As though he were watching a movie flashback he next saw himself back in that cold, dirty basement, his head cradled in Laryssa's arms. He watched her, or rather *sensed* her, pleading with him not to go, he felt her tears on his face, heard her declare her love for him and plead for forgiveness. The thought that she actually wanted and needed him to live filled him with joy. He felt his eyes tingle with incipient tears and thought that that was curious since he didn't even have a body, much less eyes.

Michael in some sense "knew" that he couldn't leave his daughter now after having just found her. All this he was thinking and experiencing, but it was as if the thoughts and experiences were happening to someone else. He had the sense that he was being instructed to stay with Laryssa and that he was receiving those instructions as if they were impressed upon his mind without him actually thinking them.

The Holts and the Hoffmeyer family gathered in the hospital waiting room, a space crowded with anxious friends and relatives of other patients. They managed to find seats in a corner that isolated them somewhat from the rest of the room. They were all quite in the dark as to what had happened, having no information other than Danny's adumbrated account in his call to Loren. Danny had quickly explained to Loren that he, Carlos, and Michael had gone to Gardonez's place and found Laryssa who was probably, Danny was pretty sure, at the same hospital as Michael. He also added, without supplying much detail, that there was gunfire, that Michael was gravely wounded, and that he and Carlos were in police custody.

The group in the waiting room talked among themselves in muted voices until at length a solemn physician emerged from the operating room where Michael was undergoing emergency surgery and explained that they weren't sure he would make it. The bullet that struck above the clavicle didn't do serious harm, but the bullet he took to the chest had done a great deal of damage, he'd lost a lot of blood, and twice they thought he'd slipped away. Both times they managed to bring him back, but his condition was very grave. Even so, they believed that if they could get him through the next twelve hours they had a chance of saving his life. The surgeon promised he'd let them know if and when there was any change in his condition.

John arrived a few minutes after the physician had returned to the OR, and Caleb filled him in on what the doctor had told them. After a few minutes John left for the police station to meet the CSR lawyer and see what could be done about getting Carlos and Danny released on bond. He knew they'd be anxious for word on Michael, and he was eager himself to learn the details of what had happened that resulted in Michael having to fight for his life. He told Caleb he'd be back as soon as he could.

There wasn't much they could do at this point so Loren suggested that they pray and asked everyone to stand and join hands. The prayers included not only a fervent intercession on behalf of Michael but also thanksgiving for Laryssa's rescue.

When they sat down again Caleb began to speak.

"You know, Michael prayed with us in our living room last week that Alicia and Laryssa would both be found. It's a bit jarring to think that if I hadn't persuaded Willis to join me for a tour of the church campus this morning Loren would never have noticed that Margarita was missing from her women's group. If he hadn't noticed her absence and remarked on it, we never would have gotten Gardonez's name. If we hadn't gotten his name Michael may never have found Laryssa. It's a bit overwhelming. It all seems like an answer to those prayers."

It occurred to Olivia that Laryssa, who was under police guard elsewhere in the hospital, was probably frightened for her father and may have had no way of finding out what his condition was. There was nothing more to be done in the waiting room so she suggested to her husband that they see if they'd be allowed to talk with her. Loren had a badge that identified him as a clergyman so they were fairly confident they'd be given permission.

When they arrived at her room she was being examined by doctors who had decided to keep her overnight. She was sedated so the Holts were unable to get in to see her, but her mother, a woman named Julia, had been called and was on her way to the hospital from Philadelphia. Loren and Olivia chose to wait until she arrived so they could tell her what they knew of Michael's condition and offer whatever solace they could. They realistically didn't think they'd have much opportunity to talk with the mother since she hadn't seen Laryssa for nearly two years and had long since assumed she never would again, so she probably wouldn't be much interested in speaking to anyone but her. Even so, they stayed.

⚜

About a mile across town five friends of the Gardonez clan were seated around a greasy kitchen table bespattered with the accumulated stains of several months' of spilled food and drink. The apartment was in a state of filthy disrepair. The soiled dishes and cutlery from the last week or so cluttered the sink, and the trash receptacles were stuffed to overflowing with beer bottles and cans. Snack food bags, some only half-empty, were strewn about the kitchen. Music, to which no one was listening, played loudly on a radio in another room. Cockroaches scuttled across the floor, but no one paid them any heed until one dropped from the ceiling onto the table whereupon it was promptly squashed with the bottom of a beer bottle.

The friends at the table were all men, they were all violent, and they were all furious that Roberto and another of their friends had been killed, a third seriously wounded, and four others, counting Enrico, had been taken by the police. It was word of all this that had brought these men together around this table to discuss how they might avenge their companions' deaths. But first they had to find out what happened, and for that they'd have to wait until they could talk to their *amigos* in police custody. That might take a while.

They did know several facts, however, which they'd gleaned from neighborhood witnesses who had gathered when the ambulances and police pulled up in the aftermath of the shootout at Roberto's apartment. They learned that *two* men had been wounded and taken away, evidently to different hospitals since the ambulances left in different directions.

They knew, too, that one of the wounded men was an African-American, probably in his late thirties or early forties, and thus not one of them.

They also had been told that two white men, one of whom had a short, military style haircut and the other of whom had a pony tail and might have been Hispanic, had been taken away by police along with three of their fellow gang members.

One thing they didn't know was that one of the men sitting around the table with them was a snitch.

CHAPTER TWELVE

The clock in the hospital waiting area was showing 11:05. The room was relatively quiet except for a fussy baby whose harried mother was there because another of her children had swallowed a serrated bottle cap.

Loren and Olivia had returned to the waiting room from Laryssa's hall, having talked briefly with her mother and filling her in on the scant details, so far as they understood them, of what had happened that evening. They also explained to her what the doctor had told them about Michael's condition.

Julia was overwhelmed with emotion that Laryssa had been found and was in satisfactory condition despite the awful treatment she'd received from Gardonez and his friends. Her joy was damped, though, by anxieties over Michael's precarious status. She still loved him even though she felt she couldn't live with him given that he had chosen careers, first the military and then CSR, which were not only dangerous but which took him away from home for such long stretches at a time. She thanked the Holts and promised to let them know when Laryssa could have visitors. They, in turn, promised to let her know of any further word on her ex-husband's health.

By the time they returned to the waiting room Patty had taken Alicia home, and John had just returned from talking to the police and his lawyer. He reported that he'd been unable to speak with Danny and Carlos, but their lawyer told him they weren't going to be released, at least not tonight.

John shared what he was able to coax out of the police on the events of that evening and explained that the house where Laryssa had been kept was inhabited by men quite likely involved in narcotics and from time to time a little sex-trafficking on the side.

"How widespread is this sex-trafficking, and how much of a problem is it in the United States?" Olivia wanted to know.

"Human trafficking in general is an extremely lucrative trade," John explained. "In fact, it's the third most profitable illicit industry after drugs and counterfeiting. It nets about $99 billion a year.

"Most of the sex traffic in this hemisphere is women being sent north into the states from places like Tenancingo in Mexico, but occasionally it goes the other way, as it did with Alicia. Her case was unusual as well in that she was not a runaway, but abductions like hers happen from time to time. We were very lucky to have had the house in Mexico under surveillance when she showed up there."

John glanced at Caleb who was nodding his head slightly. "Alicia was taken only because this drug runner in Mexico named Felix Castro put out the word that he was interested in an Anglo girl for his personal use and would pay handsomely for her. In fact," John concluded, "she may have pretty much been kidnapped almost by accident since these people usually prey upon runaway kids who sometimes aren't even missed."

"John, I'd like to ask you a couple of questions about Alicia's rescue." There were some matters that Caleb wanted very badly to have cleared up and he might not have another opportunity.

It was CSR's policy to share no information on operations and tactics with anyone outside the company, however, and John was very reluctant to say anything at all. There could be all manner of unpleasant legal consequences if the wrong people got wind of the wrong information, but whether he thought tonight's shootout would be the end of the road for CSR or whether he was just fatigued from the lateness of the hour, the stress, and all of the hectic running around, he chose to be a little more forthcoming with Caleb than he might otherwise have been. He told him that he'd answer what questions he could.

Caleb fixed his eyes squarely upon John's and began to speak. "John, talk to me about what happened in Mexico. How did Carlos and Danny and the others find Alicia and get her back? Did they have to hurt anyone?"

John glanced quickly at the Holts who were listening intently for his response and decided to give Caleb the bare minimum. As soon as he did he realized he shouldn't have.

"Yes, Caleb, there were some people hurt. It was unavoidable."

Caleb lowered his eyes briefly and then asked softly, "Was anyone killed?"

John nodded, more with his eyes than with his head, but said nothing.

"Was anyone tortured?"

Caleb wasn't aggressive or demanding. His voice was gently courteous, almost hushed so as not to be overheard by others in the room, and John could tell it wasn't merely superficial inquisitiveness that prompted the questions. He sensed that Caleb harbored a deep-seated concern that his joy at having regained his daughter had swept the moral questions surrounding her rescue into a mental closet from which they were now reemerging.

"No, not exactly." John was being forthright, but he feared that the "not exactly" would only heighten Caleb's curiosity and elicit another question. It did.

"Can you explain the, 'not exactly,' John?"

His question floated in the air like wisps of cigarette smoke until John gave an almost imperceptible sigh and began to formulate an answer.

"The team had to convince a man who had information on Alicia's whereabouts that he *would* be tortured if he didn't give that information up. I guess the expectation of torture is a kind of torture itself, but no one actually caused him any serious physical pain."

"But if the man hadn't given the information on Alicia would your men have actually tortured him?"

John thought the exchange had gone far enough and that Caleb had been given sufficient insight into what happened for him and the Holts to digest and try to reconcile with their moral convictions.

"I'm sorry, Caleb. I've already said too much."

Caleb nodded. He was almost relieved that John hadn't answered his last question. It would have made his inner struggle more difficult than it already was.

"I understand. It's just that I'm so thankful for what you guys did on the one hand, and on the other, I'm afraid that the way you did it goes against so much of what I believe. I just don't know what to think. I'm very conflicted." He smiled grimly, and the look on his face gave expression to the moral quandary he wrestled with and which seemed to have no easy solution.

John sat back in his chair and clasped his hands together over his stomach. He started to speak and then stopped, substituting instead a sympathetic nod.

                                                      ভ

It was 2:40 a.m. The Holts and the Hoffmeyers had gone home, and John had dozed off in a chair in the waiting room. He was in a light slumber when a doctor emerged from the OR and stood in the doorway as if weighing whether to wake him. John awoke on his own, sparing the surgeon further deliberation, and looked up at him expectantly.

"He's resting. There's no more that can be done now. We'll know more later. He's being moved to Intensive Care." John thanked him, and the doctor retraced his steps through the door from whence he'd come.

John thought that he may as well go home, but his home was an apartment outside Washington where he had lived by himself since he and his wife broke up five years before. He was too tired to make the drive in any case, so he decided to keep vigil in the hospital until the doctors could tell him something more definitive. Meanwhile, he sent out a lengthy text to all CSR personnel, some of whom were halfway around the world, explaining the situation and his concern not only for Michael but also for the future of the organization he had founded and built.

At 1:10 the next afternoon a nurse from Intensive Care found him in the chapel with Julia and Laryssa, who had been released that morning. All three looked at the nurse without saying anything. There was no need to speak. Their anxious expressions voiced the question for them.

The nurse pursed her lips before beginning. "The doctors think he has a good chance of pulling through, but they caution that his condition could still deteriorate. At this point, though, they're more optimistic than they were last night. He's apparently pretty tough."

Her words produced deep sighs of relief, hugs, and a measured optimism. It seemed the worst was over, Michael was in the hands of some of the finest doctors in the world, and there was hope.

Several hours later, Danny and Carlos were processed out at the police station. Their lawyer had posted bond, they had no prior criminal history, and both had exemplary military service records, which helped win their release. John stood alongside as the paper work was completed, and the four men exited into the late afternoon skies and brisk chill air of an early December cold front.

Their intention was to drive over to the hospital to check on Michael's condition and then go to dinner.

In the noisome apartment not very far from the hospital the late Roberto Gardonez's five friends were awaiting word from their sources on the street. They wanted to know where the wounded African American had been taken, who his two accomplices were, and when those accomplices would be released from police custody.

By 2:00 p.m. they'd learned from a friend of a hospital orderly that the wounded man was at Johns Hopkins, which confirmed what they'd already surmised. By 5:30 p.m. they were informed that two men who fit the description of the hospitalized man's associates had been released on bond from the police station. They assumed correctly that these men would eventually go to the hospital to visit their friend.

One of the men in the apartment was selected to drive to the hospital to watch for two visitors who conformed to the description they had of Roberto's assailants. If these men were seen going into the hospital the lookout was to call the others who would

drive over and exact their revenge in the parking garage where they assumed, again correctly, that the men would have parked their car.

By chance, the man they chose for the task happened to be the informant. His name was Cesar.

It was cold and dark by 6:30 p.m., but the plaza in front of the main hospital entrance was brightly illuminated. Cesar had been pacing around the plaza for an hour waiting for someone to show up who fit the description he'd been given. He was also wrestling with a difficult dilemma.

On the one hand, he felt a certain tribal loyalty to his fellow gang members, a loyalty based to no small extent on fear of what they'd do to him if he let them down, and on the other hand, he also felt a different kind of loyalty to a certain Sgt. Jenkins of the Baltimore City Police Department who had in the past rewarded him handsomely for tips that helped the police prevent his colleagues from carrying out a few of their most egregious activities. He knew that if he tipped Jenkins on this one substantial benefits would accrue. He knew, too, that if his brothers in the gang succeeded in murdering the men they'd targeted he'd be an accessory and might well go to prison for a long time.

Like Hamlet, of whom Cesar had surely never heard, he was deeply conflicted, but in Cesar's case, unlike Hamlet's, his vacillation was between fear and profit.

Suddenly, all his preoccupations evaporated. Four men were approaching the hospital entrance and two of them fit very closely the description he had of the men involved in the shootout at Roberto's. Cesar followed them inside and got close enough to eavesdrop on their inquiries at the Information Desk. He could hear them asking if they'd be permitted to see a patient by the name of Michael something or other. They were told that the patient couldn't have visitors, but they could go up and talk to the nurse on his floor if they wished. He also heard the lady behind the desk tell the four men that there were security police stationed at the patient's room, and anyone who tried to enter would be stopped. The men elected to go up and speak with the nurse.

Cesar was convinced that two of these men were the ones he was instructed to watch for. It occurred to him that he could just ignore their arrival and report that no one had shown up, but he didn't. On an impulse, impulse being the guiding principle of his life, he took out his phone and texted his companions, alerting them that the men they wanted to kill had shown up at the hospital.

He then spent several minutes strolling around the spacious foyer trying to make up his mind what to do about Sgt. Jenkins. It eventually occurred to him that he was in a win/win situation. Having tipped off his friends, his "cred" with them had surely risen, and if he tipped off Jenkins as well, he'd score big with him, too. He called Jenkins' number.

Jenkins was just about to go off-duty and head home when he received Cesar's call. He wasn't sure what to make of it, but the snitch told him there was a hit soon to go down at Johns Hopkins hospital, probably in the Orleans St. parking garage. Jenkins jumped in the first Ford Crown Victoria Police Interceptor he could find, called for backup, and raced for the hospital with lights flashing and siren screaming.

⸎

The patient couldn't receive visitors, the nurse explained, but she did disclose to Michael's friends what she could of the extent of his wounds, the nature of his treatment,

and his prospects for recovery. They asked her a few questions and left the floor about fifteen minutes after having arrived.

Emerging from the main entrance into the clear, bracing night air, they crossed the plaza, then Orleans Street, and walked briskly into the parking garage opposite the hospital. John's Grand Cherokee was parked on the second level near the middle of a row of cars. As the four men approached the Cherokee their attention was riveted by the piercingly loud squeal of tires seventy five feet behind them. A car was careening around the corner and heading straight toward them at high speed.

The CSR men all turned toward the sound and knew immediately what it meant. Four men were visible in the car. John yelled

"Guns!" and all four dropped to the pavement between John's car and the vehicles on either side just as the men in the car opened fire. The assailants' car, a black Nissan, was going too fast for its occupants' aim to be accurate, and a half dozen bullets thunked into the surrounding automobiles or ricocheted loudly but ineffectually off the concrete.

Tires shrieked again as the driver of the Nissan tried to brake and back up to afford his accomplices cleaner shots.

John quickly opened his car's door and reached into the glove compartment to retrieve his .357 magnum.

⚜

Just before the mayhem erupted in the garage Sgt. Jenkins sped into the plaza in front of the hospital and spotted Cesar standing at the hospital entrance peering intently toward the garage across the street. Coasting up beside his snitch he cast the man a questioning look. Cesar looked around, nodded silently with his eyes and head in the direction of the garage, then turned and walked away.

With lights and siren warning off traffic Jenkins cut across Orleans Street and roared into the garage. Peeling tightly around turns at the highest speed at which he could still retain control of his vehicle he emerged onto the second level and immediately beheld the gunmen showering a parked car with bullets as their Nissan sped past their crouching targets. The Nissan lurched to a stop after traveling another twenty yards and the back-up lights came on.

What next took place lasted only twenty seconds, but seemed to everyone involved to last much longer.

Jenkins floored his Police Interceptor, hurtling it toward the Nissan to block it from backing up.

Despite the siren and red and blue flashing lights the driver of the Nissan, probably in a state of semi-panic from the excitement of the moment, apparently didn't realize soon enough that a car had driven close up behind him. He crashed into Jenkins' Interceptor causing the doors on both vehicles to fly open and the air bags to deploy. Jenkins drew his Glock 22 semi-automatic, climbed free of the cruiser, using the door as a shield, and screamed at the gang members to drop their weapons and get out of the car. They complied with his second command, but not the first.

As they clambered from their vehicle several of them opened fire at Jenkins hitting him twice in his bulletproof vest. The impact of the first bullet staggered him, the second knocked him down, but he was able to return fire striking one assailant in the chest and forcing the others to seek cover in front of their car.

Jenkins regained his feet, but a bullet skidded off the concrete, striking him in the tibia. The shot shattered the bone, knocking his leg out from under him, causing him to fall hard on his back. His hand smashed against the garage floor when he fell sending his Glock flying from his grip and spinning across the pavement to within reach of Carlos who was kneeling behind a car only a few feet away.

Danny had spotted the Remington 870 shotgun in the front seat of the squad car and dove head first through the open passenger side door, pulling the gun from its brace, and pumping a round into the chamber as he lay across the seat. Windshield glass was flying all around him, and bullets ripped into the upholstery above his head. He popped up and fired the shotgun through the shattered windshield at the first target he spotted. He couldn't see what effect his blast had,

but he could hear a man in evident pain scream a string of obsceni-
ties in Spanish.

Carlos jumped out from behind his car, grabbed Jenkins' weapon
from the pavement, and positioned himself protectively between the
Nissan and the now vulnerable and helpless police officer. John also
had his revolver in hand, and Danny, John and Carlos directed a with-
ering barrage of fire at the two remaining threats crouched behind the
front of their car. Within moments both men raised their hands into
the air shouting, "*No mas. No mas.*" The CSR men stopped shooting.

Amazingly, though Sgt. Jenkins suffered a painfully fractured
tibia and chest contusions, no one from CSR was hurt. Their lawyer
had engine oil smeared all over his suit from squeezing his prone
body as tightly against the greasy concrete pavement as he could,
and John's Cherokee was riddled with bullet holes, but that was the
extent of the damage.

Of their attackers, two were gravely wounded, the one shot by the
police officer would not survive, and one of those who surrendered
had a non-life-threatening injury. The other was unhurt. Sgt. Jenkins'
backup arrived just as the gang members were raising their hands in
surrender, and a team of paramedics soon followed to take Jenkins
across the street to the ER.

While John and his lawyer explained matters to the police, Carlos
and Danny sat on the glass-littered pavement with their backs resting
against Jenkins' Crown Victoria, exhausted in the aftermath of the
adrenaline rush and resigned to be yet again taken into police custody–the second time in just under 24 hours.

Danny propped his elbows on his knees and buried his face in his
hands. "If that cop hadn't been here or if those shooters had gotten

here five seconds sooner, we'd all be on our way to the morgue right now," he observed wearily.

"Somebody's trying to tell us something, I think," Carlos muttered, "and we're not doing a very good job of listening."

CHAPTER THIRTEEN

One week later Caleb and Patty hosted a dinner party for Willis and Marie and the Holts. It was an act of thanksgiving to their friends for their unflagging support during those terrible dark days spent sitting together for long hours surrounded and taunted by despair and fear. It was also the first chance they'd had to relax and talk together since the night in the hospital.

Their house was gaily decorated with Christmas greens, lights, and pine-scented candles, creating a festive atmosphere in stark contrast to the gloom which pervaded their home just a few weeks earlier.

The three couples sat down to a wonderful meal skillfully prepared by Patty and her husband. Alicia had eaten earlier and after a perfunctory appearance to greet the guests she retired to her room to do homework. Caleb and his wife had recognized that Willis and Loren seemed to be growing more comfortable with each other, and appeared even to be developing a friendship. Caleb knew his brother enjoyed the company of thoughtful people, people who liked to discuss ideas, even if he didn't agree with them. Willis once told him that there are only so many opportunities for conversations with interesting people and that he didn't want to miss any. Caleb hoped that bringing Loren and his brother together again would foster good conversation and perhaps nurture their nascent relationship along.

Marie, on the contrary, didn't particularly care for the Holts. She was polite, of course, but she was nonetheless a woman whose atheism had inclined her to the ideas of Marx and Darwin, and the Holts seemed to be precisely the sort of people who stood in the way of achieving the secular progressive state she envisioned. The future, as she saw it, lay in unfettered scientific naturalism and socialism, and Christianity of the sort espoused by Holt was the last remaining impediment to both.

Caleb asked Loren to offer a blessing, after which the group chatted over appetizers about the attempted assassination of the CSR men at the hospital, a subject on all of their minds, and after having said all that could be said on it they jumped desultorily from topic to topic until about half-way through the meal they returned to the events involving CSR at the Gardonez's apartment, the hospital garage shootout, and the rescue of Alicia.

"You know," Caleb said softly, glancing around the table at his guests. "CSR rescued five other children besides Alicia on that one mission." He had learned this from John when they spoke at the hospital the night Michael was shot.

Murmurs of admiration circulated around the group as Caleb continued.

"Patty and I are certainly thankful to God and to those men that Alicia's back, but it puts us in a tough dilemma. We're thankful to men who may have lied and used torture to bring our daughter back safely and, as if that's not bad enough, when I talked to John at the hospital he as much as admitted that they even killed some of the men who held Alicia. I've been struggling with this ever since he told me. Even *before* he told me, actually, since I suspected it was the case from the first day they showed up here at the house. They violated everything I believe about how people should treat others, but maybe the worst of it is that in my heart I'm glad they did it, I'd want them to do it again if that were the only way to save Alicia, and I feel terribly guilty for thinking that."

Caleb paused and shook his head slightly. The table was quiet.

"Then I think of all the pain Alicia's kidnappers have caused others. The heartbreak and the loss, and I can't help thinking they got what they deserved, and then I feel guilty for thinking *that*, for not being more forgiving and merciful."

"You're just human, Caleb," Patty consoled him.

"I'm *too* human. I have a long way to go, I guess."

"We all do, Caleb," Loren assured him. He was himself wrestling with some of the same thoughts Caleb was. Was it wrong to do what CSR did to get Alicia back? Would it have been wrong to have *not* done it?

Caleb exhaled a sigh of resignation and turned toward Loren, sitting to his left, with an expression that sought from his pastor some guidance and consolation.

Loren hesitated and then let out an inaudible sigh of his own. "The boundaries we place on our moral beliefs, Caleb, are maybe like the boundaries we place on our beliefs about what's ultimately real," he glanced across the table at Willis. "Sometimes those boundaries get stretched by life. Sometimes they get completely shredded. Life often refuses to conform to our assumptions about it. It's stubborn that way."

Caleb stared down at his plate and dabbed his fork at his mashed potatoes, not sure what to make of Loren's words which seemed a bit enigmatic. He changed the subject slightly. "I thought about pro- posing to the elders that our church take an offering for Michael, or even for CSR, but then wouldn't that be an endorsement of what they did?" He turned again to Loren as if to solicit an opinion, but Loren wasn't sure that this was a good time to discuss that particular idea.

Fortunately, Caleb didn't really expect an answer to his question. No sooner had he asked it than he was moving on to another aspect of his daughter's rescue. "Apparently, Carlos and Danny and the rest of their team were able to find out how Alicia wound up in Mexico. Somebody like the bunch they got in that gunfight with grabbed her off the street and sold her right away to a trafficking ring. The traf- fickers flew her to Arizona and she was smuggled across the border through an underground tunnel and within twenty four hours she was in the house that CSR had been watching for a couple of days. It was just luck that they found her."

"Not luck–an answer to prayer," Patty gently corrected her husband.

Caleb nodded and continued his narrative making eye contact all around the table. His words were deliberate and solemn. His fork hovered above his dinner but seldom touched his food. He was too engrossed in the details he was divulging to pause for a bite while he was relating them.

"John had also been talking to Laryssa, and she told him that after Enrico Gardonez had been arrested Laryssa overheard Roberto talking on the phone telling other men to come over to the house. When it got dark they were going to move the girls because it was too risky keeping them there. She heard Roberto say that maybe it was time to hand them off to the traffickers who, John said, would prob- ably have taken them to another city and set them up in prostitution.

Laryssa apparently resisted being moved which provoked Roberto to beat her, which is when Michael and the others intervened."

Olivia mentioned how lucky the men were not only at the apartment where Laryssa was held but in the parking garage as well. It seemed almost miraculous that none of them were killed.

"I can't imagine what it must be like to be shot at," Marie remarked offhandedly, reflecting on what the CSR crew confronted when they entered Roberto's basement. Her comment prompted a furtive glance from Olivia out of the corner of her eye at Loren. Loren reciprocated and lightly bit his lip as his eyes returned to his roast beef. Marie had unwittingly summoned a memory in Loren of an episode from several years ago that few people besides Olivia knew about.

Loren had visited a lady, a single mother in her late thirties, who'd been attending services at his church. This poor, beleaguered woman had an abusive, violent nineteen year-old son over whom she had no control whatsoever and of whom she lived in constant fear. Loren sat in her living room on a tattered sofa trying to offer what hope and comfort he could while running through some options with her.

As he was explaining what help she might receive from various social agencies the son appeared in the doorway with two of his comrades. It was the middle of the day in the middle of the week, but none of them looked like they'd had to take off work to be there, and they all looked like they were either high or at least mildly intoxicated.

The son glowered threateningly for a couple of seconds at Loren and then without shifting his eyes from him demanded of his mother a reason why this white man was in his house. Mom tried in a soothing but tremulous voice to explain that Loren was a preacher, and that he was just visiting to talk about his church. The situation was very tense and the tension was exacerbated by the fact that the young man seemed highly volatile and, worse, Loren could see a gun in his belt.

The son announced that Loren's visit was over and demanded he get out, "*now*." As Loren rose to comply, the son lit into his mother, berating her for bringing a white preacher into the house. Loren said goodbye to her and made his way past the son and his two surly friends toward the door. As he reached the doorway he heard the mother, mortified by the disrespect with which her son was treating a clergyman, imploring him not to be so mean. That seemingly reasonable request, however, triggered an outburst of screaming and physical threats from the young man that terrified his mother and brought her to tears. Loren was sure the young thug was going to beat her just as the woman had testified to Loren that he'd done in the past.

Holt didn't know quite what to do, so he hesitated in the open doorway, but he realized that he couldn't just stand there and watch the woman get verbally, and maybe physically, slapped around. He had to do something, so, with more boldness in his voice than he actually felt, he advised the son that there was no justification for his behavior and admonished him to treat his mother with more respect.

Enraged by this white man's impertinence the son wheeled, drew his gun from his belt, and fired in Loren's general direction. Fortunately for Loren, the shooter was not entirely sober, and the bullet struck the door frame about six inches from his shoulder.

Holt was so startled by having been shot at that he staggered backward through the doorway and tumbled down the front steps as another bullet whizzed by his ear so close he thought he could feel its draft.

For some peculiar reason the words of Winston Churchill popped into his mind at that instant. "There is nothing so exhilarating,"

Churchill once remarked, "than to be shot at with no effect." Notwithstanding the great man's opinion, Loren didn't feel exhilarated at that moment. He scrambled around the corner of the house, embarrassed by what seemed to him to be cowardly flight, but what else could he do? Having ascertained that no one was pursuing him he took out his phone and called 911.

The police arrived in a few minutes and took the son into custody. He eventually went to jail for a while. His mother later told Loren that when they sent him off to prison it was the safest she'd felt in six years, but she was fearful of what would happen once he was released.

Loren was yanked back from his reminiscence of this sad and frightening incident by Marie's voice. She was lamenting the miserable state of the city's poor, the contemptible trade in young women, and the cheapness so many attached to other people's lives. She shook her head in disgust and dismay at how much remained for government to do to bring all men to the place where they treated women, and each other, with respect.

"It's so…," Marie was groping for the right word to describe her revulsion at people who would treat young girls the way those men treated Alicia and Laryssa, "It's so *hideous*."

There was a momentary silence following Marie's assessment until Olivia spoke up. "There's a lot that's hideous in the world," Olivia agreed, "and I don't think it'll get better until men reconcile themselves with God. Man's rebellion against God is what makes the world ugly."

Marie, of course, didn't think much of Olivia's opinion. She didn't think God had anything at all to do with anything men do. "Well, that's one view, I suppose," she sniffed. "Others see things differently." Marie's voice oozed both condescension and passion. "What must be done is to get people out of poverty and educate them on how to properly treat their fellow human beings. We need to improve our penal system so that it actually rehabilitates people instead of making them worse. We need to minimize the disparity between the haves and the have-nots, and we need to invest more in improving the quality of life of people who might otherwise go down the wrong road, to expose them to great art and literature and the more beautiful things in life."

Loren was deeply skeptical that the moral cancer he believed to be metastasizing throughout the culture could be cured by spending more money on it, but he didn't want to get into a political debate with Marie. In his mind it wasn't a political problem. It was spiritual. Undeterred by Marie's dismissal of his wife's opinion he canvassed the table with his eyes, speaking softly but with obvious feeling.

"Well, maybe we do need some of those things, Marie, but I think Olivia's right. The only way we'll ever make a dent in the world's ugliness is by loving people the way Christ modeled it for us in the gospels. Art, music, literature, and nature all make human existence more beautiful, at least at their best they do, but if we really want to make the world a better place the best thing we can do is commit to truly loving our neighbor."

Willis and Marie each frowned at their dinner plates as Loren spoke. He didn't want to make them uncomfortable so he added a final thought he assumed they could all mostly agree on.

"Every act of kindness is like a note played in the symphony of a person's life. Hopefully, when we get to the end of life we've created something truly beautiful. And maybe enough people will join us along the way so that we have an entire orchestra performing a magnificent symphony." Loren smiled, pleased with his extemporaneous metaphor. "The Russian writer Dostoyevsky once said that beauty will save the world. I think he meant something like that. 'Beauty,' he said, 'is the battleground where God and the devil war for the soul of man.' Whether you take that literally or metaphorically I think there's a lot of truth in what he says."

Willis took a sip of wine, set his glass on the table and changed the subject. "Loren, don't you ever doubt? Don't you agonize over the possibility that what you tell people on Sunday morning is just wrong? That it's all a fantasy?"

Holt looked across the table at Willis. Of course he had doubts. Everyone does, unless they're a fanatic, but he'd come to realize that doubting one's convictions is not a bad thing. It was for him a motivator prodding him to learn more, to dig deeper, to understand things more fully. In his experience doubt was the stimulus that nourished his intellectual growth and deepened his understanding of his faith. Even more than that, though, the central claims of Christianity were to him so beautiful, so compelling, they'd done so much to change his life and that of so many others, that he committed himself to them unreservedly, despite whatever doubts might assail him from time to time.

"Sure, Willis. There are times when I wonder if I'm really right about this or that detail, but on the fundamental question, the question of God's existence, it'd actually be very difficult for me to doubt that. Whenever I read about how the brain works or look at the sky on a clear night it just seems so obvious to me that there's a powerful intellect behind it all. Life is so marvelously designed, the universe is so vast, so exquisitely fine-tuned to permit conscious beings to exist that the notion that it all happened by blind forces and coincidence is literally incredible to me."

"Don't you think, though," Willis persisted as he placed his knife and fork across his plate, "that the vastness of the universe should count *against* the belief that it was created by an omniscient deity?"

Loren sat with his hands folded in his lap. Willis' question made him curious. It seemed counterintuitive, and he was interested in hearing him elaborate on it.

"Don't you think that the fact that it's so unimaginably huge and we're so incredibly tiny makes us completely insignificant? We're just a speck, a grain of sand on an infinite expanse of beach. Why would a God create such a huge universe just for us? I mean, it seems awfully wasteful of him and awfully egocentric of us to think that it's all so that we might exist for a relative split-second of cosmic time. If God created the universe for us, I should think he could have done it far more economically and much more quickly than the thirteen billion years or so it took him to do it."

Loren leaned forward and dabbed the corner of his mouth with a napkin. "Well, I think it's a mistake to argue that man's significance is somehow diminished by the size of the universe, Willis. It's like insisting that the collisions of subatomic particles in that Large Hadron Collider in Switzerland are insignificant because the collider is so much bigger than the particles. I read somewhere that the thing is seventeen miles in circumference and took ten years and about nine billion dollars to build. That's a lot of resources just to produce those microscopic collisions, but those tiny collisions are the whole reason that enormous machine exists."

Loren laid his napkin on the table and speculated that maybe the universe *has* to be as vast as it is in order for it to produce and sustain us.

"After all, if God used the Big Bang to create the world, then in order for all the elements that make up living things to exist, entire generations of stars would need to be born and die. It would take billions of years for elements like carbon and oxygen to be formed in the cores of those stars and then be thrown into space when the star died and eventually coalesce in the form of a planet from which living things could be fashioned. All this time the universe would've been expanding. In a way, it has to be as old as it is and so as big as it is just for us to be here at all.

"Besides," he added, "God has infinite resources. No matter how much he expended on creating the universe, it isn't wasteful, he still had plenty left over, and anyway, I don't think we only exist for a split-second of cosmic time, Willis. I believe we exist forever. The only question, at least for me, is what kind of existence we'll have during that eternity."

"Loren," Patty asked as she and Caleb began to clear the dinner plates from the table and set out a dessert. "You said that beauty would save the world. How does God fit into that?"

Loren hesitated briefly, twined his fingers in front of his chin, and lifted his eyebrows.

"Well, beauty is part of God's nature, Patty. It flows from him like light flows from the sun. It exists because he does, and it's one way he displays himself to the world. Everything he does is beautiful.

"Then what about love?" Olivia asked as she sampled Patty's apple raisin pie.

"Love and truth are each a different type of beauty," Loren conjectured. "Love, or goodness, which may be the same thing, is *moral* beauty. Truth is *epistemic* beauty. Jesus Christ is a pure expression of both love and truth, which is one reason he's beautiful. In fact, one reason the gospel has had such a powerful attraction for people over the centuries is that it's a beautiful love story, a story that's been the inspiration for so much of the artistic, musical, and literary excellence we treasure in our culture."

On a conscious level Marie thought that Holt's description of Christ, and in fact his whole exposition at the table, sounded a bit overwrought and ludicrous. Nevertheless, like a barely perceptible breeze gently rustling the leaves of a tree, his words stirred something inside her. Subliminally she found herself wanting to hear more. If she'd been aware of this she might have attributed it to a wish to probe for errors in his thinking, but maybe that wasn't really the reason at all. His talk of love and beauty had struck a chord in her heart even if she wasn't fully mindful that it had.

Willis leaned forward to place his napkin on the table. "It's a shame more of his followers today don't follow his example. Maybe more people would be less inclined to reject the faith if they saw more people actually living it."

Loren smiled and shrugged slightly. "Maybe so, Willis, but I think a lot of people see what they want to see. In any case, love isn't easy. Christ calls us to fill the world with beauty by loving others, but it's a very hard thing to do. Anyone can love people they like and admire and who seem to have life all together, but to treat people with dignity when they insist on living in squalor, to treat them with respect when there's little about them that seems worthy of respect, to treat them with kindness even though they make you angry and frustrated, that's what God tells us to do. It's not treating people one way to their face and another behind their back. It's not just loving people who agree with us on religion or politics. It's not just loving people who are grateful to us for what we do for them. There's no virtue in any of that. It's too easy."

The table grew quiet until Olivia offered that maybe that Russian writer should've said that *love* will save the world.

What Loren had just said about the difficulty of loving the unlovely moved Caleb to share a perplexing lesson in human nature he'd learned from his own experience. He finished chewing on a piece of pie and gave voice to the thought, jabbing the air with his fork for emphasis.

"One of the disappointments–maybe *frustrations* is a better word– in the work our church does in the city is that sometimes the people we help don't seem to appreciate it much. Sometimes they act as if they think they're entitled to it. It's really hard to love people who're like that. Maybe it's human nature, but when people don't have to do anything in return for the help they're given, they sometimes take the help and resent you for giving it."

"Well, it's not hard to understand why, I suppose," Willis suggested. "When you help someone, in a way, without wanting to, you make yourself superior to that person, and the sense of inferiority the person feels causes them to be resentful."

"I guess so," Caleb replied and went on to explain to Willis and Marie that that was why in their work with the poor they always insisted that people do something in return for what they're given. It makes them feel they've earned the help and that it's not just charity. It preserves their dignity.

Loren nodded and quietly elaborated on Caleb's idea.

"Yeah, in fact we tell our volunteers that if they expect people to be grateful for what they do, or if they expect their efforts to change the way people live, they're in for a lot of disillusionment, and they're going to burn out. Our task isn't to change people, it's to love them. It's a hard lesson to learn, I guess, it's a hard kind of love to master, but it's the love that moves the sun and the stars."

"Dante," Willis observed. "Last line of *The Comedy*."

Loren smiled and flicked his eyebrows in tacit acknowledgement as he carved off a small piece of pie with his fork and raised it to his mouth.

Marie had been impassive throughout much of this conversation. It wasn't that she disagreed with what was being said so much as that she didn't understand what God had to do with one's ability to love people. She was torn between being repulsed on the one hand by Holt's attempt to smuggle God in as a motivator to love others when he certainly wasn't needed nor welcome, at least not by her, and being seduced, on the other hand, by the emphasis he claimed Christianity places on love and beauty and the irenic way he made his case.

A recollection popped into her mind. She remembered reading with considerable irritation an essay by an atheist, no less, who reluctantly admitted that most of the cultural advances made in the last two thousand years were directly attributable to the Christian worldview. Hospitals and universities, art, architecture, and music, charitable organizations and a belief in human rights and equality under the law all arose, this writer claimed, from the conviction, mistaken though he thought it was, that the universe was the product of a Creator who made man in His image, who loved all persons, and who invested in each one the right to be treated justly. This conviction led men to make laws that codified justice for everyone and inspired them to produce art that glorified their Creator.

She recalled, too, Holt's argument at the reception celebrating Alicia's safe return in which he maintained that our sense of moral obligation and our belief that our lives can be genuinely meaningful are both empty fantasies unless there really is a God.

Then there was a scholar she'd heard on public radio who insisted that modern science owed its existence to the Christian belief that the universe, having been created by a rational God, was not itself divine, and thus no sacrilege was committed by studying it. Moreover, believing the world to have been created by a logical mind, early investigators assumed it was an orderly, logical place, governed by laws, and that its secrets could therefore be discovered by the exercise of their reason. Apart from this belief science would never have gotten off the ground, and in fact didn't succeed anywhere else but in the Christian West.

The impression Marie had gained from all this, much to her disgruntlement, was that Christianity was to science and culture what the booster rocket is to the space shuttle. It's what lifted the whole thing into orbit. Marie summarily rejected the idea as nonsense when she first encountered it, but the more she read and thought about it the more she realized there may be something to it. That didn't bring her any closer to thinking Christianity was true, of course, but it was disconcerting to think that a Christian worldview was a *sine qua non* for the social and scientific progress we've made over the last two millenia.

She was fascinated by these thoughts even as she chafed at them. They crossed her mind like the words of a chyron scrolling across a television screen, and she was absorbed in trying to deny to herself that there was really anything to them. She imagined herself as one of those cartoon characters with a demon on one shoulder and an angel on the other, each taking turns whispering in her ear. What she couldn't decipher was whether Holt was the demon or the angel.

Musing on all of this had made her appear distracted and preoccupied, an appearance Loren incorrectly interpreted as indifference or antipathy to the course of the conversation. He didn't wish to antagonize her by seeking to involve her in a discussion he thought she resented, so he directed a question instead to her husband sitting directly across from him.

"Let me ask you something, Willis. Are you familiar with the British writer, Julian Barnes?"

"Sure, he's an atheist."

"Yes. In one of his books he poses an interesting question. I'd like to hear your thoughts on it."

"Okay, go ahead."

"I'm paraphrasing, but it goes something like this: Would you rather that when you die there is nothing, and you turn out to be right, though you wouldn't know it, of course, or would you rather that when you die you find that there really is a God who offers you an existence of eternal love, happiness, and wonder, as Christians believe?"

Willis tried to think of ways to finesse the question, but realized what he was doing and rebuked himself for attempting to evade giving a straightforward answer. He knew what Loren was getting at. The question was simple: Would he prefer there be nothing but annihilation at death or would he prefer to emerge, like a butterfly from its chrysalis, into a new life of eternal happiness underwritten by a loving, omnipotent Deity?

"Well," Willis answered after mulling it over for a moment, "anyone would prefer the second circumstance I guess, but unfortunately I just don't think it's rational to believe that that's the way things are."

Loren scraped the last bit of pie onto his fork and held it over his plate.

"I'm not sure that everyone *would* prefer the second circumstance, Willis. I think atheism is a kind of wish-fulfillment, at least for many people it is, anyway. They don't *want* there to be a God so they refuse to believe there is one."

Loren's statement broke Marie from her reverie. "Why would someone *not* want God to exist?" She asked incredulously. The way she saw it, whether someone wanted God to exist or not wasn't really relevant. Even if someone did want God to be real there's a huge step between wanting him to exist and actually believing he does, and that was a step neither she nor a lot of people she knew could manage.

Before Loren could respond to her question Willis preempted him.

"You know, you might be at least partly right, Loren. Now that I think a bit more about this it's probably true that a lot of atheists really don't want God to exist and in my mind they have good reason for not wanting him to exist. As I reconsider your question, it may be that *I* don't want God to exist either."

"Why not?" His brother asked with a bemused expression.

"Look. I want to be able to live my life without having to conform to what some higher being dictates. I don't want the universe to be the kind of place where I don't have the freedom to determine my own life. I don't want to be a slave or a pawn in some cosmic plan in which I have no vote. If God exists then we lose the one thing that gives us dignity–our freedom to choose. I prefer to have dignity in this life even if it means that I cease to exist at death, which, I guess, means that I prefer that there be no God."

"In other words, Willis, you see God as infringing on your autonomy, and you resent that," Loren summarized.

Willis contemplated Loren's interpretation of his words for a moment. "Yes, I suppose that's right."

"But how does God take away your autonomy? You're still free to live whatever kind of life you want, aren't you? God doesn't stop you from choosing whatever it is you choose."

"No, but if he threatens me with punishment for breaking his laws I'm not really free to disregard him, am I?"

Loren considered Willis' answer for a second before answering.

"Okay, but you believe yourself now, as an atheist, to have the kind of freedom you want, don't you?"

"Pretty much, yes."

"But you embrace a 'scientific' view of the world that reduces man to atoms, makes him a slave to physical forces, and strips him of the ability to make genuine choices. If anything deprives man of his autonomy, Willis, it's the mechanistic, *scientistic* picture of humanity you accept that leaves no room for free will.

"Besides that, you're not really autonomous in the sense you wish to be, anyway. You're still threatened with punishment by the state if you transgress its laws. Yet you're willing to submit yourself to the authority of the state and its sanctions. If you're willing to subordinate your freedom to a government of morally imperfect men, why would you think it so unreasonable to subordinate your freedom to a morally perfect God?"

Loren smiled. "You know, it always puzzled me that people are willing to lay their freedom at the feet of other men, men who are often tyrants, but the thought of laying their freedom at the foot of the cross is repugnant to them. I guess I just don't get it."

"Well, I don't get why anyone would want to hand over his freedom to a man, a peasant actually, who lived two thousand years ago," Willis replied with a smile of his own. "That doesn't make sense to *me*."

"But do you agree," Loren countered, "that it *would* make sense if that peasant was in fact a manifestation of the creator of the universe, the one who made us and loves us and desires what's best for us?"

"Maybe it would, if I granted you your hypothetical that God exists and that Jesus was in some sense God, but I don't. I just can't believe that. It's so implausible as to be impossible for me to believe. It's literally incredible to me to think that there's some unseen world out there populated by spirits and deities. It's a primitive super-stition, and

without wishing to sound insulting, I'm surprised that smart, edu-cated people still cling to it." Willis smiled to take the bite out of this last remark. He didn't want to sound like his colleague Watkins back in the faculty lounge, and he didn't want anyone at the table to be offended by his opinion.

"I understand that that's your view, Willis, but, also without wishing to be insulting, I'm wondering whether you hold that view because it follows from your desire that the world *not* be the kind of place where there's a God who loves us and who guarantees us life forever because that God might place restraints on how you might otherwise choose to live your life."

Marie was slightly uncomfortable with the repartee between Loren and Willis, but when she asked herself what about it, exactly, made her uncomfortable, she couldn't come up with a specific answer.

Both men were cordial and polite and treated each other with respect so there was nothing about the way they presented their cases that was unpleasant. Maybe part of it was that she was coming, grudgingly, to respect Loren's position, or at least Loren himself, a lot more than she thought she would and this was unsettling. She set her misgivings aside and waded into the exchange herself. There was something she wished to add to it.

"Pastor"–For some reason she had difficulty calling him by his first name. Perhaps the familiarity of that mode of address implied a fondness she hadn't heretofore felt–"I don't wish to offend either, and maybe it's impolite to say this as a guest in Caleb and Patty's home because I certainly don't want them to take it the wrong way, but views such as you're promoting tonight are dying out around the world, at least in the enlightened parts of it. Don't you feel that you're fighting a losing battle, that you're on the wrong side of history?"

Loren's face assumed a wistful expression as he conceded with a slight nod of his head that Marie may well be right. There were many times in his life when he thought that the cultural slide away from the beliefs he held had turned into an irresistible, irreversible juggernaut. The image that came to his mind was of a vast throng of people racing in the dark across a plateau, unknowingly rushing toward a deep canyon. He couldn't stop the mad, suicidal rush of the culture, but he could place a few bridges across the abyss that might help some cross safely to the other side. That was, in any case, his hope and the work to which he'd committed his life.

He looked away from the table and then back, settling his eyes amiably on Marie's. "You might be right about that Marie, but that's probably what they said about Christians in first century Rome, too. In any case, I think it's better to be on the wrong side of history than on the wrong side of truth. If embracing and trying to live by what I'm convinced is true puts me outside the mainstream of the culture, then so be it. Truth is too precious to forfeit just because it's not fashionable."

Gradually the conversation moved on to other topics, and the three couples talked late into the night. Eventually, it was time to leave. Marie continued to find herself strangely bothered by the dinner discussion throughout the remainder of the evening and especially during the drive home. In the car she indulged in some outspoken psychological introspection, using her husband as a sounding board.

Why was she so resistant to the idea of God? What was it about that idea that had repelled her so viscerally for her entire adult life? Was it the *idea* of God, was it God himself, or was it the obnoxious people she sometimes encountered who believed in God? But surely her in-laws were two of the finest people she knew, and even the Holts, she had to admit, were good people, even if all of them were regrettably misguided. Now she was beginning to wonder, though the possibility struck her as unthinkable, whether they really were misguided or whether it was she and her husband who had been wrong all these years.

When Willis heard her half-whisper that she wondered why she was so resistant to God the painting in Loren's office depicting Christ knocking on a door that only opens from the inside, the door the artist described as representing the "obstinately shut mind," sprang immediately to his own mind. The scene the artist portrayed impressed itself vividly upon him as he navigated the city's streets.

Was that painting in effect a portrait of Marie and himself? Were they obstinately shut to a truth that was standing just outside their hearts but which they stubbornly refused to acknowledge? Were the distractions of life and his desire not to submit to any authority that would demand he give up some of his autonomy preventing him from hearing the knocks on the door? He didn't think so, but he couldn't dismiss the image from his mind. As Marie talked he kept seeing that painting, except in the mental image of it he formed, he was in the painting, sitting just on the other side of the closed door, engrossed in a novel, deaf to the light-bearer rapping softly at the portal.

Marie was saying, mostly to herself now, that she always assumed that Christian belief was an atavism, a silly superstitious holdover from a more primitive epoch in history, and that the enormity of the world's suffering amounted almost to a proof that no benevolent deity could possibly exist. The whole church thing seemed to her to be a sham, and she was repelled by the widespread opposition among Christians to both abortion rights and gay marriage, notwithstanding her fondness for her in-laws, who were unpretentiously opposed to both.

It occurred to her as these barely audible thoughts tumbled steadily from her lips, one following hard upon another, that in the conversations with Holt to which she'd been a party she never heard him use the word "religion" or talk about any of the beliefs she found to be most odious. Nor, as she thought about it, had she ever heard Caleb or Patty do so.

One thought kept spawning another like cells rapidly dividing under a microscope. She wondered how she would've answered Julian Barnes' "would you rather" question, and how she would've responded to Holt's questions had he asked them of her rather than of her husband. She didn't know, and for reasons she still couldn't quite pin down, she was disturbed by it.

She was troubled, too, by the sense she had at that moment, for no reason she could discern, that she was desired, that she was deeply loved. Maybe it was all a delayed reaction to all the talk back at dinner about love and beauty, but for perhaps the first time in her adult life she was consciously examining the underlying motives of a religious skepticism that for decades she'd taken for granted as the only reasonable posture of an intelligent, well-educated person. It was a disconcerting, disorienting experience.

EPILOGUE

I n the months which passed since the events culminating in the violence in the hospital parking garage, some in the local media, specifically a coterie of journalists who had once been described as having a tendency to see the best in the worst of people and the worst in the best of people, did what they could to discredit and besmirch the CSR team.

Their initial ploy was to portray the episode at Roberto's apartment as a racial hate crime, an effort in which they were augmented and abetted by opportunistic political activists and politicians. The strategy was beginning to gain traction among the general public, especially in the less affluent communities, when it was discovered that Michael, Laryssa and Dominique were all African-American and Carlos was Hispanic. When those unwelcome facts surfaced the racism strategy quickly unraveled.

Undeterred, certain members of the media and their allies next turned to painting the CSR members as a bunch of fanatical right-wing vigilantes. This slander seemed to enjoy some promise of success until it came to light that Roberto had imprisoned Michael's daughter for two years, and Dominique for several months, and had repeatedly raped, beaten, and otherwise abused both of them. Hard upon these revelations the public learned that it was these same CSR men who had rescued Alicia Hoffmeyer, whose plight the whole city had known about. The vigilante charge against CSR only enhanced their mystique and burnished their image, much to the frustration of those who were intent upon their undoing.

Finally, an attempt was made to salvage something of value from the notoriety of the episode by turning the shootings and deaths into a cry for stricter gun laws. This tactic also fizzled, however, when it was pointed out that none of the guns used in the shootout at Roberto's apartment were possessed or carried legally under Maryland law, and that stricter laws wouldn't have made any difference.

Indeed, there was such a vociferous public backlash on behalf of the CSR team, especially after the attempt on their lives in the parking garage, that the politicians, always gauging the direction of the winds of popular opinion, began to talk as if they'd been ardent admirers of the CSR men from the very first. The media, too, mindful of their ratings and financial bottom line, began to back off, and the District Attorney ultimately decided not to file charges against Michael, Danny, or Carlos, who were being hailed by the citizens of Baltimore, and in fact across the country, as American heroes.

The future of CSR, however, was in limbo. The unwanted publicity they'd received would make it very difficult to continue their mission in the U.S., and John was thinking about moving the operation offshore or overseas. They also feared retaliation from the criminals, both in Mexico and in the U.S., whose lives they'd made difficult.

Danny assured John that he'd stay with the company wherever it relocated. He believed in the work and felt he was on the side of the angels in fighting the evil of human trafficking. If there is a God, he told Carlos, he was sure God would approve.

Michael pulled through his medical crisis due in large part to the expert care of the doctors and nurses at Johns Hopkins, and Julia added to his good fortune by agreeing to start seeing him again if he promised to get a normal job. A petroleum drilling company in North Dakota offered him a position managing security in their burgeoning new business, and he happily accepted their offer. He was scheduled to start as soon as his rehab was complete.

His strange experience in the hospital operating room had mystified him and led him to seek out Loren's counsel. He had no idea what to make of what happened to him. Was there a completely natural explanation for it or was it an experience for which no scientific account was possible? He had no idea and neither did Loren, but talking about it led the two men into several serious and fruitful discussions about God and eternity.

With a job lined up, Julia thought that dating seemed to be a somewhat pointless deferral of the inevitable and offered to remarry Michael without any further ado. A small service, at which Loren was asked to officiate, was planned for just after New Year's day.

Laryssa was in the midst of counseling to help her cope with the aftermath of her terrible ordeal at the hands of the late, unlamented Roberto Gardonez. Holt's church was helping with the expense and other details. The thing that most promoted her healing, she told everyone who asked, was her parents' decision to get back together. Despite what she had endured, her heart was buoyant at their reconciliation. She planned to finish her GED in North Dakota and maybe go to college there.

Carlos chose to take a sabbatical from CSR, live with his parents for a while in California, and prepare for a future very different from his past. Like Michael, he received job offers from all over the country, one in fact from the same firm that hired Michael, but he felt himself destined for holy orders in the Catholic Church and decided that he'd been resisting the call for too long.

It was odd, he thought, because he never considered himself particularly pious or devout, but something in his visit with Loren Holt, he had no idea what, caused a switch to flip somewhere inside him. It was as if his soul was a tuning fork that vibrated in resonance with Holt almost from the moment he walked into his office. When he read the lines of the poem on the office wall about the Hound of Heaven pursuing his "prey" he could almost feel the vibration silently pulsing inside him.

In the days and weeks since that otherwise unexceptional meeting he grew increasingly sure that serving God through serving others was what he was meant to do with the rest of his life. He'd already made inquiries into the process for becoming a priest and was anticipating the next steps toward that goal. The Hound of Heaven appeared to have finally chased him down.

With information provided by CSR, and through the interrogation of Enrico Gardonez, the trafficking ring was largely rolled up in Baltimore, Washington, and the outskirts of Cuidad Juarez. There were numerous arrests in both the U.S. and Mexico which resulted in the identification of Alicia's kidnappers. They were found to have been two of the men in Roberto's apartment the night Laryssa was rescued, one of whom was shot and killed by Carlos and the other the man apprehended in the car with Dominique.

Felix Castro was also arrested. Three girls were found imprisoned in his house at the time of his arrest, though none of them was American, and his drug business was dealt a serious blow.

Luis was sentenced to ten years in prison but would probably not serve even half of that. Carlos came up with the idea of writing to Luis in jail. Maybe no one is so lost, he thought, that the Hound isn't interested in them.

Loren had given Willis and Marie a couple of books he'd hoped they'd read. They didn't refuse them, which was heartening, and they even told Caleb that they might come to church with him and Patty one of these Sundays. They both thought they'd like to hear a sermon or two from Pastor Holt. Loren was as delighted as he was surprised when Caleb told him this. He assumed that Willis, and especially Marie, had very little time for anything remotely related to a church. A few months previous he would've been correct.

Caleb expressed his concern that Marie's hostility toward Christianity was more psychological than intellectual, that her own awful life experiences had caused her to sour on the idea of God as a loving father. Caleb feared her attitude toward God was an implicit renunciation of her own father and stepfather.

Loren wasn't sure. He knew his own youthful rebellion wasn't due to an unfortunate father/son relationship and he assumed that neither was Willis'. Maybe it's different, Loren speculated, with fathers and daughters. Interestingly enough, one of the most famous examples of filial renunciation in the history of Christianity actually went the other way. Caleb expressed an interest in the example so Loren recited the story to him.

"Francis of Assisi had given up a life of carousing and debauchery and embraced Christianity," Holt began. "From that point on he chose to serve and identify himself with the poor in his dress and manner which embarrassed his wealthy, domineering father, Pietro de Bernardone, who on one occasion dragged his son into the main square of Assisi and publicly beat him. He also had him locked up for a while in a storage room."

"Sounds like a pretty dysfunctional relationship," Caleb observed.

"Yeah, well, it gets worse. When Bernardone, who was a successful cloth merchant, discovered that Francis had sold some of his fabric to pay for repairs to a local church, he was incensed. He hauled him before the bishop and demanded his son be made to compensate him for the merchandise. Francis surprised everyone by appearing at the court, held outside the cathedral, dressed in one of the finest of his old costumes and promised to repay his debt to his father immediately. He then disappeared into the church, stripped himself completely naked, stacked the clothes in a neat pile, placed a purse of coins on top, and carried the whole package outside to the bishop in full view of numerous witnesses in the piazza. He then addressed the crowd, renouncing his sonship to Bernardone and declaring that henceforth only God was his father. As the bishop hastened to wrap his cloak around Francis, Bernardone took the clothes and money and left."

"Francis sounds like a real eccentric," Caleb remarked with admiration.

"He was. It's a strange story, but Francis was a strange man. Yet he was one of the greatest figures in the history of the Christian church. The 14th century Italian artist Giotto did a famous painting of the incident for the basilica of St. Francis in Assisi. It's titled, *The Renunciation of Worldly Goods*. It could've been titled *The Renunciation of His Worldly Father*.

"Anyway, Marie's difficulty with Christianity *may* be due to her past, Caleb, I don't know, but I guess what I'm trying to say is that not all rebellion against God is due to a bad relationship with one's father and not all bad relationships with one's father result in rebellion against God."

"That's good," Caleb replied. "Maybe Marie will wind up a little like St. Francis. Maybe Willis, too." Both men smiled at the prospect.

Over dinner one evening in early February, Olivia and Loren were discussing a situation with one of his assistant pastors that required his attention. The television was on in the living room, the local news was on the screen, but the Holts weren't listening until they overheard the newscaster state that there would be a segment on after the commercial break about the shooting in the parking garage at the Johns Hopkins hospital two months earlier. The couple left their dinners at the table and walked into the living room to see what it was about.

The news was that a Sgt. Jenkins of the Baltimore Police Department was being recognized for his valor in preventing the murders of the CSR team and had just been asked by the mayor to say a few words. Loren and Olivia sat down on the sofa to listen as the officer, an athletic-looking African-American in his early to mid-thirties, bashfully approached the microphone.

He spoke nervously, clearly not comfortable in the public spotlight, and obviously not sure what he should say. He leaned on the crutches he still needed while the shattered leg bone slowly mended, and looked directly into the camera, having finally settled upon his remarks.

"When I was a kid," he began haltingly, "I was involved in something pretty stupid that hurt a man. I felt bad about it, and I went to his house to apologize. It turned out he was a preacher. He told me that I was really a good kid and that he hoped that throughout my life whenever I was tempted to do something wrong I'd remember that I was a good person and that I should always do what good people do even when it's hard. He said that the more times you do the right thing the easier it is to do it. Those words stuck with me ever since and have sort of been a guide for me in my life. I guess what happened in the parking garage just came naturally from a lot of years of trying to live up to that man's confidence in me."

The policeman's words piqued Loren's memory. His story sounded vaguely familiar. When the officer was done speaking the broadcast returned to the news team in the studio.

"That was police Sergeant Keyvon Jenkins whose heroism saved the lives of four men targeted for murder by Baltimore gang members last December."

As soon as the couple on the sofa heard the officer's name the recollection of that night over twenty years ago when Loren was assaulted on the sidewalk in front of their house came flooding back to both of them.

Loren and Olivia stared at each other in open-mouthed astonishment. They were stunned. Loren's face broke into a wide grin as he shook his head in near disbelief. All he could manage to say was "Gosh."

"You never know, honey," Olivia said proudly, placing her hand on her husband's arm. "You never know when some little thing you say or do makes a difference to someone for the rest of his life. Just think about that, Loren. What that policeman just said was that, in a way, what you told him over twenty years ago helped save the lives of Carlos, Danny, and John."

Both of them laughed. Olivia put her arm around Loren's neck and pulled him closer. She could see tears beginning to well up in his eyes. He smiled, leaned toward her, gave her a kiss, and told her that he loved her.

CPSIA information can be obtained at www.ICGtesting.com
Printed in the USA
LVOW10s1609230915

455410LV00016B/1282/P